MINE WITH EXTRA LIME

IRENE BAHRD

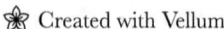

To anyone who ever felt like they were not enough.

You are extraordinary, magnificent, exquisite, and will change the world. Your goals might take longer than expected, but whatever you do, don't give up. You'll get there.

CONTENT WARNINGS

By reading this book, you may experience the following side effects:

- May make panties wet.
- May want to leave your significant other, in search of your own Dylan.
- May change your Love Language to "words of affirmation."
- May feel impulsive need to purchase a bookcase with a ladder.

You're welcome.

All joking aside, this is a slow burn, second chance **romantic comedy** with on-page explicit scenes. It is intended for mature audiences.

Additionally, there are on-page scenes with:

- Praise (directed at FMC)

- Discussion of and scenes that include submission of the FMC (_not_ a dom/sub relationship)
- Hand necklaces (no breath play)
- Impact play (hands only)
- Sensory deprivation (sight)

Please Note: Your new bestie, Emma, has an autistic child who has an off-page sensory meltdown. This is addressed from a parent POV, and autistic adults were consulted in my portrayal and discussion of Aiden. There is also discussion of IEP (Individualized Education Plan) meetings, which for some people will not give them warm fuzzy feelings. Finally, Emma's sister, Charlotte, is neurodivergent. She isn't a central character in this book, but she will be our leading lady in book 4 in the series getting her own happily ever after. Representation matters!

PLAYLIST

"I Knew You Were Trouble" — Taylor Swift
"Never Really Over" — Katy Perry
"Perfect" — Ed Sheeran
"Won't Go Home Without You"— Maroon 5
"Wrecking Ball" — Miley Cyrus
"The Reason" — Hoobastank
"Jealous" — Nick Jonas
"Water Under the Bridge" — Adele
"The Scientist" — Coldplay
"Head Over Feet" — Alanis Morisette
"A Thousand Years" — Christina Perri

1

EMMA

"Is this your first mixer?" I can't fault my new boss, Susan, for trying to gauge exactly how much marketing experience I have. I'm only twenty-one, and while I didn't embellish my resumé, my experience is more in management than marketing or sales—definitely not networking.

"Oh, no, this isn't my first," I lie as our car approaches the mixer where I'm likely not qualified to represent her company.

As I step out of the car, I become increasingly nervous. *What am I doing? I don't know how to network!* Luckily, another account executive, Katie, is already here to hold my hand through it.

She meets us at the car and whispers, "You've got this, Emma," as she links her arm with mine. "Just walk in, grab a glass of wine, and keep to yourself this round. The goal is to get to know everyone. People want to do business with someone they like and they're going to *love* you! Watch what Susan and I do, and you'll be fine."

I blow out a deep breath, only to stop dead in my tracks as we cross the threshold into the mixer. *Is everyone here over sixty-five?* Katie squeezes my arm once before heading to the open bar across the room. I follow a few steps behind her and pick up a glass of whatever wine is being served. After a quick taste, I'm sure the varietal is just "white wine." While I'm no connoisseur, this is definitely something that came from a box. I should be careful; I don't want to be hungover tomorrow from a glass of cheap chardonnay.

Katie wanders over to one of our existing clients, who gives her a tight hug, then with a warm smile shakes the hand of the person next to them.

Man, she's good at this.

Sipping my sad excuse for wine, I scan the room. After a minute of not recognizing anyone from the chamber of commerce listings, I spot a gorgeous, tall man with dark hair and glasses. He can't be older than twenty-five, making us two of the youngest people here. I have absolutely no game when it comes to men, but I do know that I should *not* be staring at him for more than a few seconds, especially since he hasn't taken his eyes off me.

I tear my eyes from the stranger, searching for Susan or Katie, finding they're both entertaining other attendees. I make my way to Katie, hoping for an opportunity to learn from her. Meanwhile, I can still feel the mystery man's eyes on me. It's making my heart race and stomach flip.

I sneak a quick glance to see if he's still looking my way. He absolutely is. My cheeks are warm, and I can try to convince myself it's from the wine, but it's from the attention of the most attractive man I've ever seen. His ability to make my breath hitch from a single glance is too much to handle at a professional event.

Get it together, Emma!

Our gazes meet again, and I need to find out who the hell this guy is. As I reach Katie, I interrupt as professionally as I can, "So sorry, can I steal Katie away for a few moments?" She looks at me with intrigue, and as we walk away after excusing ourselves, I lean in and whisper, "Hey, who's that guy over there?"

She looks to our left. "The younger one with glasses?" I nod. "I don't know. I haven't seen him before, but *damn*, he can't take his eyes off you! Shoot, I wish I had a guy who looked at me like that."

I double check as stealthily as I can, and his intense gaze is still focused our way, sipping his drink. He's hardly paying attention to the men he's standing with.

"Go introduce yourself! You're single and he's checking you out like he's moments away from finding a dark corner and having his way with you."

"I could *never!* That's way too forward. Plus, we're here for work," I insist. I consider walk over to the bar to escape this whole thing, but remain rooted in place when notice he's excusing himself from the two men he's talking to and heading in the same direction.

So much for escaping.

"Oh my God, Emma! Yes, you can. Wait, it looks like he might beat you to it. Quick, tell me something funny." Katie's eyes are twinkling with delight, which only makes me more nervous. I'm pretty sure I've become her entertainment for the mixer; no good can come from this.

"Katie, what the heck? I'm not funny, and what do you mean he might beat me to—"

I feel his presence like an electric charge filling the air before I hear him. "Hi there. Hope I'm not interrupting?" His voice is low, practically a purr, and shiver runs up my spine as I turn around.

"Oh, hi. Um, of course not! We were just, uh... talking shop."

Who the hell says "talking shop?" Come on, Emma, do better! Focus...

How can I, though? He's one of the most beautiful men I've ever met with the most adorable dimpled smile, dark blue eyes that pierce my soul, and I'm wrapped in his scent of leather and embers. *Or maybe that's just the name of the candle that I bought on my last Target run?* I blow out a deep breath; it's criminal how attractive this man is.

Oh, shit, how long have I been staring?

I'm pulled from my thoughts as he hands Katie and me a glass of wine. "I noticed you both were running low."

Katie declines, "Oh, I don't accept drinks from anyone other than a bartender, *but* I am Emma's ride, so she can have mine. I have to make sure she gets home safe."

I smack her arm and turn back to him. "I... yeah, sure, thanks." I'm unable to get the words out as he pours one glass into the other and hands it to me. As I take it, our fingers brush. An innocent touch, but it causes goosebumps to erupt all over my body.

Does he feel that too? I sure as hell did.

"I don't think we've been properly introduced," I announce with as much confidence as I can muster. "I'm Emma, and this is Katie. We work for a local magazine."

He holds out his hand and I take it. *There's that zing again.* "Dylan. It's a pleasure to meet you, Emma. I haven't seen you here before, is this your first time?" His lack of acknowledgement of Katie isn't lost on me—all his focus is on me.

"Yes, but Katie has been before." His eyes never leave mine, even at the second mention of my coworker. The energy in the room is heavy; I don't know what it is about this guy, but I feel a pull toward him and can't look away.

Katie clears her throat, likely uncomfortable with whatever *this* is. "Okay, right, so I need to check on a few people. It was great to meet you, Dusty."

"Dylan," he corrects.

"Right, Dylan. Emma, I'll find you later." She winks at me and I wince in embarrassment. Hopefully he didn't catch it.

Who the hell winks at people?

"I'm sorry, she's... well, that's Katie," I admit sheepishly. I'm not sure what to say, but I desperately need to fill the silence. "So, Dylan, what brings you here tonight? What do you do?"

He brings his drink to his lips and his gaze hasn't wavered once, remaining on me like we're the only two people in the room. "Investments."

That could mean literally anything, could he be any more vague?

Dylan takes out a card from his wallet and hands it to me. "My personal number is on the bottom. It was great to meet you, Emma." Disappointment stabs me in the gut as he walks away, glancing over his shoulder with a dimpled grin. Brushing off the interaction as purely professional, I place the card in my purse, and set down my too-full glass of wine to find Katie. I need to get the hell out of here before my cheeks get any redder.

"So, how did it go?" Katie teases. "Did he ask you out?"

"I don't want to talk about it." He's easily the most handsome man I have ever met, but it's more than that; I feel a gravitational pull toward him that I can't explain. Except, I may have imagined it all.

———

The next day as I arrive at the office, Katie greets me at the door with two cups of coffee. Bouncing with excitement, she hands me one and asks, "Did you call him? Did he call you?"

I set the coffee on my desk, shrug off my coat, and take a seat. Powering up my computer, I sigh, "No, I didn't call him. We just met *last night.*"

She eyes me suspiciously, sipping her own drink. "Call him *now!* What are you waiting for?"

What *am* I waiting for? I can easily call his work number under the guise of a business call. I hate that it's dishonest, and what would I even say? *"Hi, it's Emma, we spoke for like 2.5 seconds and I think you're incredibly attractive. Want to hang out sometime?"*

Instead, I tell her, "Maybe tomorrow, I need to catch up on emails." Focusing on my computer to avoid her gaze and persistent matchmaking, I check my schedule for the day. "I have a luncheon *and* another mixer today?"

Katie doesn't even blink. "Yep, and Susan wants you to go to both."

"Seriously?" I sigh and bring my coffee to my lips for the first time, forgetting that Katie takes her coffee black. I wince at the bitterness and set it down. "Fine, I'll go, but only because there's a full bar at this one."

Katie laughs and leaves my office while I dive into work for a few hours.

At tonight's mixer, there's a much younger crowd. Susan sent Katie and me alone this time, but since I'm still learning the ropes, I really have no business being here without her.

We grab a few glasses of white wine right after we arrive. Unfortunately, the advertised full bar is all well liquor. I don't need to be praying to the porcelain gods because of a bottom shelf gin and tonic.

"He's here," Katie whisper-shouts.

"Who?" I scan the room. Just as I'm about to turn back to her, I spot Dylan. He's laughing with a few older gentlemen and a woman. Thankfully, I don't think he's seen me yet, and I can hide in the sea of people between us. "Oh, Dylan? It makes sense. He is here to network, just like us."

"Oh, come on! This is such a cliché meet cute." Katie is way too invested in this.

"You've read too many romance novels. This is *not* a meet cute. This is not destiny, or happenstance... or whatever the hell you want to label it." I roll my eyes at her and sip my wine, which is, surprisingly, better than last night. "Who are our prospects tonight; who does Susan want us to meet?"

"You can start with Mr. McHottie over there," she jokes, gesturing to Dylan. Just as I'm about to open my mouth to protest, he looks our way. "Looks like we've been spotted, Em. Okay, so I'm going to find Matt and see if I can upsell him for the next issue. Good luck!" Katie walks away smirking, leaving me alone and a sitting duck. *Great.* I think about going after her, but I can't help but notice Dylan's also alone.

Well, there's no time like the present.

I blow out a deep breath, square my shoulders, and walk over to him. As I approach, he has the biggest smile I've ever seen—like a kid on Christmas morning. His boyish grin takes my breath away.

What is wrong with me? You're here for work.

I've never been so nervous to talk to someone before, but I muster up every ounce of courage I have, and draw from everything I learned in my public speaking and communications classes in college. *Deep breath, Em.*

"Dylan, hi." I offer a polite, flirty smile. If I have to talk to him, I may as well have some fun.

"Well, hello. Two nights in a row? Small world." Dylan brings his beer to his lips, still smiling. His eye contact is powerful but playful. "You mentioned last night that you work for a magazine. What do you do there?"

"I just started this month as an account executive, which is basically a fancy name for ad sales." I'm so nervous around him. Not only is he insanely attractive, he carries himself with so much confidence that I struggle to find my voice.

Dylan laughs, gesturing with his beer around the room. "Ah, yes, we have quite a few of those here. Which magazine? Do you have a card? I forgot to ask for it yesterday."

Is he trying to get my number? No, that can't be it.

I dig in my bag and pull one out. "Here, that's me."

Taking my card, he asks, "Is this the best number to reach you at?"

I stare for a moment, then clear my throat. "Um, yes, that's my work cell." I don't have a work cell, but he doesn't need to know that.

"Thanks." His smile meets his eyes as he pockets my card. "I'll have to give you a call when we are ready to put in an ad."

Ugh, so it's a business thing. Damn it.

To avoid his searing gaze, I use the only tool in my arsenal. "Sure thing. Well, it was great seeing you again, Dylan. Please excuse me." I hold up my phone that is most definitely *not* ringing. "I have to take this." I turn on my heel and walk away before I embarrass myself further.

With my phone to my ear, I look for Katie, willing myself not to sneak a glance at him as I retreat. I know damn well I'll find his ocean eyes on me. She's by the bar, laughing at something the guy she's with is saying. *What was his name?*

Mark? Michael? I was too distracted by a tall drink of water with piercing blue eyes when she mentioned him to remember correctly.

"Oh, Emma! You must meet my absolute favorite client, Matt."

Hah! I knew it was a M name.

Shoving my phone in my bag, I extend my free hand to shake his, "Hi, Matt, it's a pleasure to meet you." Matt is in his mid-to-late twenties, tall and blond, but only a few inches taller than me in heels, putting him maybe six foot —which is a little shorter than Dylan. He's attractive, but not really my type. *Or maybe I'm just crushing on Dylan?*

He offers to grab me a glass of wine to replace the one I downed in one gulp on my way to find Katie, but I decline, "I'm okay, thank you. I just wanted to check in with Katie before I head out."

"Give me thirty and we can leave together?"

"Sure, I can wait for you," I reply as professionally as I can, but my nerves are shot. Just as I'm about to walk away, Dylan approaches, slapping Matt on the back to greet him, "Hey, buddy, how've you been?"

Matt chuckles. "Great, it's been a while! The office hasn't been the same since you transferred. Have you met Katie and... Emma, was it?"

As I'm about to confirm, Dylan replies for me with a wide grin, his dimples on full display, "Yes, we've met a few times. Old friends now, aren't we, E?"

Shoot, now he wants to be just friends. That's worse than just busi-

ness. I've been friend-zoned! Also, E? Since when do I have a nickname?

He lowers his voice and leans in beside my ear so that only I can hear him. "When I call you, I hope you don't rush off the phone as quickly as you did with that one you took." I suck in a quick breath, unsure how to respond after being caught.

Katie jumps in, full of half-truths, "Emma was telling me that she just took on five new clients. I don't know how she makes the time to join me at these events."

"Really, Katie?" I mutter under my breath.

Beaming, she continues, "Well, gentlemen, we have an early morning meeting that I forgot about, but I'm so glad we had a chance to catch up."

Dylan's smile fades. *Is he sad I'm leaving?* We shake hands and, the moment Dylan touches me, it feels like a mild electrical current travels up my arm. My hand fits perfectly in his and I appreciate that he doesn't offer a limp handshake like some men do, simply because I'm a woman. He pulls me a little closer, his thumb gently and ever so subtly swiping over mine.

Did I imagine that?

"I'm sure I'll see you soon, Emma." His voice is silky, and I have to remind myself that this is just work; he's probably like this with everyone.

Katie and I slip away from the crowd. Once we're out of earshot of everyone, she looks me dead in the eyes. "That man wants you. Time to play hard to get."

"I am *not* going to play hard to get," I insist. "Plus, he only wants to be friends or business acquaintances."

"Friends with benefits, maybe," Katie scoffs. "Did you see him checking you out as we left?" *Was he checking me out?* "Does he have your number?"

"He has my card."

"Mark my words, he wants more than a business relationship. Just be careful when he reaches out. By the way that man looks at you, he's probably the kind of guy who jumps in with two feet."

Katie's words replay in my head the entire way home.

2

EMMA

In the last month since we first met, I've run into Dylan no less than ten more times. He sits at my table during every luncheon. Every mixer, he brings me a glass of wine or comes up with an excuse to talk to me. He *always* finds me. A few people have asked if we're dating—which is super awkward—but we always change the subject. The flirting is fun, but we're friends at best and business contacts at worst. I have no idea where we stand.

I'm in the middle of drafting an email to one of my clients when my cell phone rings with an unknown number. "Hello?"

"Hi, is this Emma?" The voice on the other line is familiar, but I can't place it.

"Yes, who's this?"

"Dylan," he says matter-of-factly, as if I should know who he is. Of course, I know *exactly* who he is, but I need to play it cool.

"Oh, hi, Dylan No-last-name," I tease. My voice feels shaky; I hope the quiver is only in my head. He lets out a hearty laugh.

"My apologies, I should've clarified. Dylan Alexander."

"Oh, hello." I clear my throat. "And how may I help you, Dylan Alexander?" I straighten my posture, even if no one can see it but me.

"I wanted to see if you were available to grab a drink or dinner to... discuss a few things."

Like a friend thing? Or a business thing? Or a date thing?

"Um, sure. I think I have a few evenings free but my lunches are all booked up." I'm a liar; I have zero lunches booked. *Ball's in your court, Dylan.* If this is a date, his next move should make it obvious.

"Perfect. How about Thursday evening, after work? Maybe 5 p.m.? I have a meeting that goes until five. Hope that's not too late?"

Well, shoot, his next move was *not* obvious. This could still be a work thing.

"Sure, that should be fine. My car will be at the train station, but I can grab it after work and meet you a little after 5:30?"

"That's not necessary. My meeting is downtown; I'll come pick you up."

Oh my God, is this a date? No, there's no way, it still feels too stuffy.

"Sure, my work address is on my card, I'll meet you downstairs when you're here," I reply. *What on earth is this man thinking?*

"Great, I'll see you then. You're sure you don't have plans?" It's an odd question for him to ask, I just told him I'm free.

"Nope, I'm available. See you Thursday."

"Can't wait." He hangs up, and I'm left gaping at my phone, wondering what the hell just happened.

———

Thursday comes quicker than I expected. When I look at my calendar, I realize why he double checked about my plans tonight—it's Valentine's Day. I still can't tell if this is a date or not, but I'm excited, no matter the outcome. I might walk away with a second date on the books, or a contract for an ad in the magazine. Win-win.

I make sure I'm downstairs a few minutes before five o'clock, surprised to discover he's right on time. Dylan pulls up to the building and gets out of his car to open my door for me. I don't know if it's possible, but is he even more handsome than I remember? I haven't seen him in a week, but it feels longer. Then, it hits me—he doesn't have a date tonight either.

On the drive to the restaurant, he asks me how my day was, and I ask about his. He rattles off some sort of stock trading information that I barely follow. So far, this outing feels very platonic. He didn't comment on how pretty I look, or do any other complimentary first date things guys typically do. I'm starting to think I read this all wrong. Maybe he's just not that into me and it's all business.

We decided to eat at a local seafood restaurant that, in my opinion, is casual enough to grab dinner as a date, but fancy enough to buy him dinner if it's a business meeting. I still have no clue what this is and suggested eating here to be sure I'm covered either way.

Entering the restaurant, the host seats us at a table in the middle of the room. Dylan sits across from me, and damn it, now I can't avoid his dimples.

As the waiter asks my drink order, I reply, "Gin and tonic with extra lime, please."

I set my napkin on my lap and look up to find Dylan with a curious expression. He pauses for a moment, his trademark dimples bigger than ever. Shaking his head with a smirk, he turns to the server. "Make that two, please." Once they leave, I ask Dylan what his look was for. He laughs to himself and replies, "Nothing. You just surprise me." I smile back, feeling a little like he's flirting with me.

There's a shift between us once we order dinner; almost all the questions he asks me are personal, like he wants to know *me*. Nothing about work. Halfway done with my drink, I decide it's time to put on my big girl panties and ask what I've been wondering all evening, "I hope you don't take this the wrong way, I just don't want to misread the situation. Is this a business dinner, or is this... *a date?*"

I bite my lower lip, awaiting his response, which feels like eternity—even if it's only a few seconds. "You're right. I'm sorry I wasn't clear with my intentions. I was actually hoping it would be a date. But if you prefer we keep things professional, I completely respect that."

"Well, I was planning on discussing potential advertising over drinks; my treat, of course. But I would be more than okay if this was a date instead." I feel a blush creeping up my neck to my cheeks.

As if his smile couldn't get any wider, I swear it just did. I've never met a man who looks at a woman the way he's looking at me. It's something movies are made of. Maybe Katie was right all along, and it was actually the perfect meet cute.

"So, to be clear, putting an ad in our magazine is *not* something you want to do?" I jest, as I continue to slowly sip my drink. I should look away, but I can't bring myself to end this staredown.

He quietly replies into his glass, "There are at least thirty things I want to do with you, and that *definitely* isn't one of them."

I nearly spit out my gin and tonic. At first, I'm not sure I heard him properly, but his eyes darken as he watches me.

Oof, this guy is trouble.

"So, tell me, when was the last time you went to a baseball game?"

I appreciate him changing the subject, the flirting is making it way too hot in here. *It's hot in here, right?* "I haven't been in a while but used to have season tickets down in San Diego when I was younger."

His boyish grin returns and my guess is he loves baseball as much as I do. "We should go sometime when they're playing up here."

"Getting ahead of ourselves, are we, Mr. Alexander? For all you know, tonight could be the date from hell, and I'll never want to see you again." I'm having way too much fun teasing him, but I swear I heard him exhale a groan when I called him that. *Interesting.*

"You and I both know how this is going to go." He's so confident, but there's so much truth to his words; I've been inexplicably drawn to him since the moment we met.

The rest of dinner is filled with laughter and "get to know you" conversation. Sadly, he brought the flirting down a notch, but I've enjoyed learning more about him. He's driven and one of the youngest in his line of business, which I relate to—being twenty-one and up for promotion after only working at the magazine for a month.

When we finish eating, he drives me back to the office; I need to grab my laptop upstairs before I head to the train station across the street. My hand moves to the handle to open the car door, but he stops me with his hand on my thigh. I suck in a breath. When I look at him, he shakes his head. "Don't you dare. That's my job." I smile at the chivalry, even if my body is on fire.

Once we're both out of the car, I know this is the moment that will make or break us. If he's an amazing kisser, I'm a goner. If he's a horrible kisser, I don't know if I can save face seeing him at events. There's something about him, though. I have a feeling it's going to be the former.

He steps toward me and takes my hand, gently caressing his thumb on top of mine. "I had an amazing time tonight." He tucks my hair behind my ear and I'm screaming inside.

"I did, too." I wet my lips in anticipation. There's a quiet moment between us before he leans forward and I lift my heels until our lips meet. The kiss is soft, gentle, but I sense he is holding back. It isn't the fireworks I was anticipating, and it isn't an epic earth-shattering kiss from my favorite books, but the flutter in my stomach is undeniable.

He steps back and opens the door to my office building for me to walk through. "Have a great rest of your night."

That's it? That's all I get?

I sigh. "You as well." I walk into my building, looking back for a moment to watch him return to his car. Maybe it was all in my head, but the chemistry I have with him is like nothing I've ever felt. I can't help feeling a little disappointed he let me go easily.

About twenty minutes later, there's a text as I'm boarding the commuter train. My heart stops when I see it's him.

> **DYLAN**
>
> I know your team isn't playing, but will you join me for a game Saturday night?

Butterflies, settle down!

I can't wait for Saturday.

3

EMMA
SIXTEEN YEARS LATER

"What? Come on! How did that not end with a happily ever after?"

Sitting at dinner with Lily and Riley, after two gin and tonics and a very long-winded recounting of my past relationship, they can't believe he wasn't *the one*. While I adore my friends, they are hopeless romantics.

"She's right, how did you not end up with him?"

"I'm not the one who ended it!" I defend. "He started dating someone else and… ghosted me." I fidget with the napkin in my lap; even after all this time, that part still stings.

"No! There's no way." I'm not surprised by Lily's rebuttal. She's the queen of optimism, always seeing the best in everyone.

"I'm serious. Out of nowhere, my calls and texts went unanswered. I later found out that he started seeing someone else, but instead of ending things, he just—*poof*— disappeared. She was prettier than me and was into golf. You *know* how I hate golf." While I love sports, I draw the line at golf. I take a few more sips of my drink, waiting for their minds to be blown at my addition.

"No, no, *no.*" Riley's fired up about my nearly two-decade-old story. "That is literally the most perfect meet cute!" Of all people, I would've expected a less enthusiastic response.

"That's what my friend, Katie, said when I first met him. Who knows, though? I probably became too clingy or something." I wave a dismissive hand. "It was ages ago." Except, it doesn't feel like ages ago… It feels like yesterday that he disappeared and broke my heart in two.

We sit in silence for a few moments, attention focused on our drinks, when Riley interrupts my pity party, "Okay, but you're divorced now, why not see if he's also single?"

It never occurred to me. To be honest, I haven't thought much about dating after my divorce to Jason was finalized six months ago, much less revisiting an old relationship. "He's probably married with a hundred kids, living his best life." I wince at the thought. It hurts to think he found his happily ever after, while I'm divorced at thirty-seven. Between work and three kids at home, I don't have time to date. "Besides, he probably doesn't even remember me."

Lily snatches my phone from the table. "I'm going to cyberstalk him!"

"Lily, please don't!" I steal it back. "The last thing I need is for you to accidentally like a photo on social media, and it will get weird as fuck."

"Are you friends on social media?" Riley asks, sipping her wine. "This just got good."

"I don't know, I'm never on there," I lie. I'm absolutely still friends with him on social media, which is why I know that he's actually married with *two* kids, not a hundred. We never comment on or like each other's posts, but I can't help checking on him every so often.

For science… or whatever.

It's been a while since I've looked, but after the divorce, I wasn't in the headspace to go down memory lane.

Riley takes out her phone and finds him under her own account. "Well, ladies, it appears Dylan is indeed unattached!"

Lily looks over Riley's shoulder, and surprises me when she asks, "Hold on, you're talking about Dylan *Alexander?*" She pulls Riley's phone to get a closer look before she continues, "I know this guy! He's friends with my husband. Dylan and his two girls even spent Christmas with us last year! Riley's right, he divorced a few months ago." She winces. "It was messy."

I was mid-drink and almost choked. "Whoa, what? You're kidding! How do you know he's single, though? Maybe he has a new girlfriend? Did Andrew tell you?" I try to tamp down my eagerness, but I'm genuinely curious how much she knows about him.

Lily smiles with pride, and a tinge of mischief. "He was in the thick of filing last Christmas and, no, he doesn't have a girlfriend. Totally single now."

Riley is still entirely too amused by all of this as she scrolls his page. "Also, everyone knows when a man changes his profile picture to his kids, things went south. See?" She shows us the timestamp on his profile picture. Her sleuthing skills never cease to amaze me. "Looks like it's been rocky for at least a year. But I'm more interested in how you guys haven't run into each other."

"I don't know," I sigh. "I haven't seen him in almost twenty years. Even if he's divorced, I don't think he has any interest in seeing me."

Riley and Lily exchange a look, then Lily places her hand on top of mine. "Only one way to find out, Em."

No, nope, absolutely not.

"That's ridiculous. What would I say? '*Hey, remember me from years ago? Heard you're single. Not that my friends cyberstalked you or anything. Up for coffee sometime to rehash the past where you ghosted me and I moved on to date men who could never compare to you?*' Yeah, I'm good, thanks." I finish my drink in one long gulp and signal to the waiter that I need a refill… immediately.

Lily tightens her grip on my hand. "No, but Dylan's special. You deserve to love again and be loved in return."

"Maybe I'll start dating again… someday. But I'm pretty sure you just plagiarized *Moulin Rouge*." I raise an eyebrow.

"So what if I did." Lily shrugs, absentmindedly stabbing her dinner with her fork. "But what if he's *the guy*? You know, your happily ever after?" I know Lily's only trying to help, but I'm so damn afraid of getting my heart broken by him a second time. I have to stand my ground.

"No, I don't think he is. Come on, what would that even look like? Two divorced parents, too many kids… It would never work."

Would it? No, why am I even considering this?

My worries lie more with bringing a man into my kids' lives than my own. My youngest, Aiden, is autistic. Between speech therapy, occupational therapy, the doctor appointments, and meetings at the school… It's a lot to bring a new person into. "I just don't think I'm in the right place in my life to date right now."

"I call BS. Aiden and the twins are doing great. Co-parenting is going well with Jason. Why are you holding back?" Lily's eyes are so full of hope it makes my heart ache. "Plus, you can't live with a nose stuck in a book forever!"

"Lily, that's *Beauty and the Beast*. Please stop referencing musicals and children's movies when discussing my lack of a love life. I promise, I'm good. Although… if he wants to give me a library, then maybe I'll consider it." I shrug.

"With a ladder!" We raise our glasses in a cheers. Lily's not wrong; it's every bookworm's fantasy.

Just when I think we've moved on from the subject, Riley grabs my phone off the table, unlocked to check on the kids. "Riley, give it back!" I yell as I swipe at her to take it back. The next thing I know, there's a ding coming from my phone, indicating a message has been sent. "Riley, what did you do?"

She hands the phone back to me. I sit there horrified; there's a new message sent to Dylan. I check for any way to rescind it. "*No, no, no!* Ugh, how do you delete it?"

They both laugh, and Riley responds, "You don't, but all I said was '*hey,*' so you don't have anything to worry about."

My face falls into my hands . At this point, I'm praying it went to his spam folder and he'll never see it.

Lily places her hand on my shoulder. "It's fine, really. He'll probably never see it."

4

DYLAN

After I finish saying goodnight to the girls, my phone vibrates in my pocket. I close the door to their room, and pull it out and find a new notification in my messenger app. I rarely use it, so it's probably spam. Almost deleting the notification, I pocket my phone. Almost. For some reason I can't explain—a gut instinct—I'm compelled to open it.

EMMA

Hey

I blink twice, wondering if it's an accidental text. *Is that even a thing?* Why would Emma be texting me at 10 p.m. on a Thursday? I haven't spoken to her in years. Surely she meant the message for literally anyone else. I'll admit, I've checked her social media profiles from time to time—*she's still stunning*—but that's the extent of it. After screwing things up years ago, she's moved on and is now married with kids of her own. My curiosity peaked, I reply.

Hi there.

A few minutes pass without a response and I resign to the fact that it was a fluke—the message was never meant for me. I make my way to the kitchen to grab a beer, setting my phone down on the counter. Water is probably a better option, especially if there's a chance she messages me back. I take one from the fridge, twist the cap off, and throw it in the trash. My phone lights up and I pause before opening it, hoping for the smallest chance that none of this was an accident.

> Sorry to bother you so late! My friends and I were at dinner and one of them got a hold of my phone. She drunk texted you. I am so sorry!

Disappointment and a pang of misplaced jealousy hits me hard; it was only a drunk text, nothing more. *Who else did they text?* Last I checked, she's married, I have no right to be jealous. I finish my water and throw the empty bottle in the recycle bin. My phone lights up, buzzing again, and I pause.

> I must sound so incredibly rude! Let me start over. Hi Dylan. Please accept my apology for my friends drunk texting you. How are you? How are the girls?

She knows I have daughters? We're still friends on social media, but that means nothing. I can't help but wonder if she's looked me up over the years. How else would she know? A wave of relief crashes over me as I read her message a second time; she might want to talk to me after all.

No, she's married, asshole. She may be your first love, but don't you dare flirt with her.

> I'm well, girls are doing great. How about
> you? How's life?

Not my best opener, but it'll do. I sit on the couch, contemplating my next move.

> We don't have to do this, I feel awful
> bothering you so late.

What does she mean? Is it because she's married? It's an innocent conversation, so that can't be it. Who knows if it's really her, or if it's still her friends messaging me. I type out a quick reply.

> The Emma I know wouldn't stand down
> from a conversation with an old friend. How
> do I know this isn't just her friends still
> texting me?

> Well, for one, we haven't spoken in over a
> decade, so I don't see how we're old
> friends. And two, I can prove it.

She sends a picture with a cheers to the camera, sandwiched between two women. *Is that Lily?* I zoom in, and sure enough, Emma's out with Andrew's wife and another woman I don't recognize. There are two limes in her drink and laugh to myself—she's still the same gin and tonic girl I knew long ago.

> A girl after my own heart, still my favorite.

What are you doing flirting with her? She's married… isn't she?

I take a closer look. She isn't wearing a ring in the photo and there's a tan line where it should be. I don't know what to make of it. Could she be recently divorced? A new message pulls me from my thoughts.

> It's still mine, with extra lime. My ex-husband hated that I drank gin, said it smelled like pine needles. So I'm in the habit of only drinking one when I'm out with the girls.

> Anyway, sorry again about my friends. Hope you have an amazing rest of your night!

She confirmed it. She's single—or at least divorced—but then why did she rush away from the conversation? I stare at my phone, wondering what the hell just happened.

Emma was always the one that got away and I'll never forgive myself for the idiot I was years ago. I had the perfect woman, and I left her for someone who wasn't half what she was. Even though I don't deserve her, if I have even the smallest chance of being with Emma again, I have to go for it.

I scroll through my contacts to see if I have her number. I don't. Why would I? It's been ages. I open the messenger app again and hover my finger over the phone icon in our chat. I pause for a few moments, take a deep breath, and hit 'call.'

5

EMMA

Moments after I put my phone in my purse, it rings, but I don't recognize the ringtone. My friends' eyes are wide. I fish out my phone. "Dylan," I whisper, more to myself than my friends. "He's… calling me?" I show them.

"Pick it up," they reply in unison.

I take a deep breath and answer the call, putting it on speaker. "Hello?"

"Hey, E. Sorry, I probably shouldn't be calling. I know you said you were out with friends." My heart stops. *Did he just call me E?* I haven't heard that in years… since him. Everyone just calls me Em for short.

All the air has left my lungs, but I manage, "No, no, it's totally fine. We were just leaving." My friends both give me a thumbs up, but it's anything but. "So… what's up?"

He pauses, then says something that feels all too familiar, a ghost of my past. "Well, I wanted to see if you were available to grab a drink or dinner to… discuss a few things." I can hear the smile in his voice. He still knows exactly what he's doing; at least Valentine's Day isn't coming up.

Lily's hand flies to her mouth as Riley whisper-shouts, "Yes!"

I hit mute and wag my finger between them. "Come on, you guys, be cool!" Unmuting my phone, I echo our conversation from nearly two decades ago, "That depends, is it a business thing or a date thing?"

He chuckles, and damn it, I feel it down to my toes. "Well, if you're currently not seeing anyone, what are your thoughts on it being a date?"

My friends are like two teenage girls who can't stop giggling. All of us are nearly forty, one would think we'd moved past crushes. My stomach is in a knot at the thought of seeing him again. I'm too nervous to say yes.

I've been quiet for too long, clear my throat, and finally reply, "I'm not seeing anyone right now, and based on your question, I assume you're unattached as well. So, sure, let's grab a drink sometime."

"Sometime? How about Tuesday? It's not Valentine's Day, but I'm sure I can plan something special."

He remembers. Of course he remembers our first date. How could he forget? I sure as hell haven't. All of the sudden, the room is too small. "Uh, yeah, sure, Tuesday works. I'll see if I can get a sitter."

What am I doing?

"It's a date. Good night, E."

I close my eyes and let the words wash over me. "Good night." I hang up and, almost instantly, my friends start talking over each other a mile a minute; I can't understand a word they're saying. "Slow down, one at a time!"

"I knew it! I knew he would ask you out!" Riley never gets this excited about impulsive decisions. As the practical one of the three of us, this is out of character for her.

"You did not!" Lily smacks Riley's arm with the back of her hand. My heart is racing and my breath is uneven, feeling like I'm twenty seconds away from a panic attack. My phone lights up with a new message in the app, making it worse.

> DYLAN
>
> Can't wait to see you. Since I don't use this app often, here's my number. 555-1234
>
> Mine is 555-5678

My friends and I leave the restaurant and hug goodbye. I promise them all of the details next time we get together, even though I know they'll be calling me the moment my date is over.

Why am I going on a date with Dylan Alexander?

The next morning, as I'm pouring my coffee, there's a new text from who I can only assume is Dylan. I don't think I saved his number after we hung up—I was a bit distracted by the inquisition of my friends.

> 555-1234
>
> How is it after sixteen years, you still take my breath away?

How could he say something like that so nonchalantly? I

haven't seen this man in ages, and yet, I can't help the smile on my face.

My son, Noah, notices. "Mom, what are you smiling about?"

I clear my throat. "Oh, nothing, it's just a good day." I hate lying to my kids, but there's no way I'd ever admit the truth. Instead, I deflect and change the subject. "Did you finish your homework?"

"Yes, *Mom*," he replies with entirely too much sass, complete with an eye roll. "Of course I did."

"Great. Can you help me get Aiden ready? We have to leave in fifteen." I pause before yelling upstairs, "Aiden! Charlie! It's time for school, let's go!" I quickly save Dylan's contact and type a reply before throwing my phone in my bag.

> Well, good morning to you too!

After getting the kids off to school, I head to work, spending the morning answering emails and being pulled into meetings that should've been an email.

Finally able to take a break at 2 p.m., I haven't eaten yet. I take out my phone to order coffee and a sandwich from the shop next door, finding a new text from a few hours ago.

DYLAN

> How's your day going? Any fun plans for the weekend?

> Sorry, I just got this! Busy day. No big plans. My son has a soccer game, but other than that, we don't have much going on.

> My kids are at their dad's on Sunday, so I plan on basking in the silence and maybe starting a new book.

He replies within seconds. It's surreal, since my calls and texts went unanswered all those years ago.

> Sunday? I don't have the girls this weekend, they're staying with my parents. Want to grab dinner and a movie Sunday evening?

Sunday? That's in two days!

I chew the inside of my cheek as I reply.

> Sunday instead of Tuesday? Sure, I'll call off the sitter.

> Don't call off the sitter. I'd like to take you out Tuesday as well.

I think back to when we first started dating; he basically asked me out for our second date before our first was even over. *Is this us starting over?* I mirror our conversation years ago, wondering if he remembers.

> Getting ahead of ourselves, are we? For all you know, Sunday could be the date from hell, and you'll never want to see me again.

> You and I both know how this is going to go.

Oh, God. He does.

This is a blast from the past. Biting my lip, I type back.

> And how is this going to go?

> Same as all those years ago. Except, this
> time I'm not going to let you go.

I suck in a breath as I repeatedly read that last text. My heart is racing at the idea of seeing him again.

No one gets over their first love. My knee jerk reaction is to run for the hills; I don't know if I can handle that kind of heartbreak again. Before I can reply, another text pings.

> Sorry, I'm not sure how that came across
> over text. I haven't flirted with a woman in a
> while, I'm a bit out of practice.

> So, you're flirting with me?

I can't help it, I want to flirt back. Flirting I can handle, as long as he doesn't doesn't become serious.

> Of course I am! How could I not? You know
> you were always the one that got away. I'm
> just afraid of messing this up again.

And, it just got serious. *Damn it.* I take a long drink of water from my tumbler on my desk and set it down. There are two more back to back texts before I can reply.

> I just want to be completely honest
> with you.

> And... I've scared you off.

> I mean, a little. But it would be nice to see
> you again, to catch up.

I don't know what else to say. He's coming in hot; I'm afraid, if he keeps this up, I'll fall for him as hard and fast as I did last time.

I can hear him out though, right? As friends?

> Can I pick you up Sunday?

> Sure, any time after 3 should be fine.

> Perfect, I'll pick you up at 5. Just send me
> the address and I'll be there.

I send it to him, then order my coffee and sandwich. It feels like my whole day has escaped me; I have only a few hours before I need to head home for the weekend. I scramble to wrap up a few projects, and before I know it, I'm out the door and in my car.

Once I'm home, I kick off my shoes and hear Lily's and my kids in my living room fighting over the gaming remotes. I avoid the chaos and head in the kitchen. "Hey, Lil, how were they?"

"Oh, you know my kids are *way* more work than yours!"

Lily's amazing, always helping me out when my childcare falls through, and is especially great with Aiden. She reminds me a lot of my sister, Charlotte; both of them are so patient and wonderful with him. Charlotte is neurodivergent herself, so I feel like she understands Aiden on a level I probably never will. I just wish she lived closer, I miss her terribly.

"Thanks again for getting them home." I open the fridge and take out a sparkling water. "So, it looks like my date was moved up."

She pauses and turns to face me with a beaming smile, entirely too excited about this whole thing with my ex. "Your date with Dylan?"

I recount the texts from him today, and she proceeds to grab her phone to start searching for date outfits for me while I finish making dinner for everyone. "You know, Lil, if this Dylan thing doesn't work out, we should just move in together." I don't know what I would do without her.

"I don't think Andrew would go for it, but you would definitely be my first choice if we wanted to spice things up." She jokingly wiggles her eyebrows and we both laugh.

Once everyone is fed, Lily heads home with her kids, then I help my boys with their homework and get them ready for bed. We're all exhausted from the long week.

Before I plug in my phone for the night, I open the text thread from earlier—*like the masochist I am*—and find a new text from Dylan. I truly am a glutton for punishment.

DYLAN

Goodnight, beautiful.

I'm going to fall for him again, aren't I?

6

DYLAN

I tuck my phone in my pocket and let out a deep breath. It's been months, but it feels like it was just yesterday that Ashley left me and the girls. I should be second-guessing jumping into any sort of relationship so quickly with Emma.

I'm not.

Even though it's been years since I've seen her, a piece of me never stopped loving her. It's just a date, but it already feels like it will be so much more.

I'm almost forty and have no interest in dating someone new. Except, this is Emma. She's not new; she was my first love. I can imagine her moving in here with her boys, us saying goodnight to all five of our kids, then staying up just the two of us, my arms wrapped around her to watch TV or read. She always fit perfectly curled up against me.

What am I thinking? I've barely spoken to her in the last decade, and I'm already fantasizing about playing house with her?

Combing my hand through my hair, I shelf those thoughts and check on my girls to make sure they're ready for bed. When Ashley left, Harriet and Lizzy asked to share a room, and I couldn't say no.

"Hey girls, ready for bed?" Lizzy is curled up in bed with a book, and her reading reminds me I left their new books downstairs. "I'll be right back, I forgot your books."

Harriet jumps up from her writing desk and stops me. "It's okay. I need a glass of water anyway, I'll grab them." She's always been the helper, even before her mom left.

"Thanks hun, are you both done with your book reports for Monday?"

She rolls her eyes at me. "*Yes.*" Harriet rushes downstairs to grab the books, and I turn to Lizzy. She's reading the fourth fantasy book in a series I'm familiar with, but I ask anyway, "What are you reading?"

She lifts the book to show me. "Come on, you know I am reading the series again before the next one is out."

Of course I know, but trying to connect with a preteen is tough. "So, I was thinking, Harriet wants to go back to the bookstore next week—something about a new fantasy book coming out. Should we all go next weekend, maybe grab a boba at that coffee place you like?"

Her eyes light up. "Yeah, that would be amazing!"

Harriet comes back upstairs with their new books and I let her in on our plans. After saying goodnight to the girls, I make my way down the hallway to my room. As I open the door, my phone buzzes in my pocket. Hoping it's Emma, I quickly pull it out.

ANDREW

Hey man, you up for catching a game on Tuesday?

You won't believe it, but I actually have a date.

I'm sorry, what? Since when are you dating?

Since I started talking to Emma.

Who's Emma?

Emma Sullivan. I dated her in my early 20s. You actually know her.

Or at least, she knows Lily.

What?

Is she the one that you disappeared on?

How did this happen?

Nevermind, it doesn't matter. No. Emma's off limits.

She messaged me by accident while out with Lily last night.

It's just a date. Why is she off limits?

If I can help it, it won't be 'just a date.'

When things go south, Lily will murder you. Hell, I'll murder you. I knew you dated an "Emma" before we met, but you said you ghosted her like 20 years ago.

You also said you had your chance and you blew it to date that blonde chick, right?

> So, all this time, when you talked about your ex... you were talking about my wife's friend?

> Seriously, you can't date her.

> Sorry, but I'm taking her out.

There's an incoming call from Andrew. I answer it, but before I even say hello, Andrew is yelling, "No! You are *not* going to make this weird. Lily and Emma have been friends for years. You're not going to mess up my marriage so you can get laid. Emma is an amazing woman! She's recently divorced and has a kid on the spectrum. You don't casually date someone like her, she doesn't need some *fling*." I have never heard Andrew so worked up over anything, other than sports. He hasn't taken a breath since I picked up the phone.

"*Whoa, whoa, whoa!* Who said anything about getting laid? I know Emma isn't like that, we're just going to catch up on Sunday."

Andrew sounds like he's choking on his drink. "Sunday? You said you can't go to the game Tuesday because of a date with her. What's Sunday?"

"Yeah, I plan on seeing her for both."

"Dylan, you're one of my best friends, but you can't do this." The fact that Lily and Andrew know Emma still blows my mind.

"You know I loved her, I wouldn't do anything to hurt her."

He sighs. "You'd risk everything. Dating Emma, you risk my friendship with her, my friendship with you, *and* my marriage. Hard pass, Dylan, I don't want anything to do with this. What makes you think you can make it work? Because, if it doesn't—"

"I have to try! Ever since we reconnected yesterday, I can't stop thinking about her." If I'm being honest with myself, I *never* stopped thinking about her.

"So, in twenty-four hours you've decided you found your soulmate? Come on, man, let's be logical about this. Emma is not the same person you dated. Neither are you. Why are you jumping into this with two feet after one day?" He chuckles. "I mean, she is *way* out of your league. So, I guess I get the appeal. You like a challenge… What am I saying? No! Don't do this."

He's right, she is out of my league, but I have to try. "I don't know, we always had this insane connection. I just want to see if it's still there."

"*Andrew, who's on the phone?*" Andrew pauses when Lily walks into the room, and I can't help listening in to their conversation. "Babe, you won't believe this, but Dylan, my buddy Dylan, who came for Christmas with his girls… *I know who Dylan is…* Right, well he's the ex Emma was talking about… *Yeah, yeah, I know, Emma and I figured it out last night. I heard all about the ghosting. Andrew, so help me, if he hurts her again…*" Lily's voice trails off, likely leaving the room. Andrew clears his throat. "Sorry, wifey walked in. You probably heard all of that, didn't you?"

"Yeah," I wince. "She doesn't seem too happy about this whole thing."

"Oh, I wouldn't worry about that, because you aren't going to date Emma, *right?* And I'm a thousand percent sure Lily is calling her and Riley as we speak." He's one of my best friends; it would be nice if he encouraged this.

"I get why you're against it, but she's everything I ever wanted in a woman. This is my second chance with her, and I'm going for it—with or without your blessing."

Andrew is silent for a moment, then lets out a deep breath. "You sound like one of those romance books Lily reads. Are you sure about this?"

"I have never been so sure of anything in my life. I never loved another woman the way I loved Emma." *Not even my ex-wife.* If there's even the slightest possibility she still feels the same way about me, I'll do everything in my power to make her mine again.

Unfortunately, Andrew's still against the idea when we hang up. He's right about one thing: I have no idea about the woman she is now. All I know is she made me want to be a better man when we were together.

Sitting on my bed, I pull out my laptop. Once powered on, I open my browser and search her name. Emma still goes by her maiden name; I don't remember her ever changing it when she was married. A quick search pulls up a few social media accounts and a website for a literary agency. She's a vice president, which I knew from internet stalking her intermittently over the years.

Falling down the rabbit hole that's the internet, I discover she's on a school PTA board, and a volunteer for an organization that funds services for autistic adults and children. I recall Andrew mentioning she had a kid on the spectrum, so it doesn't surprise me. I can't help wondering how she has time for all of this. She is incredible on paper, always has been. When I think back to how driven she was when I knew her, she hasn't changed one bit.

I lean back against my headboard and pull out my phone to open a social media app I know we aren't following each other on. When I find her profile, I scroll through photos of book promos and reviews. She hasn't posted in years, since she moved into the VP position.

At first glance, I don't think much of it, but I'm starting to see a pattern—they're almost all romance books. I click on a few of them to see what her favorites were. For the most part, she read stories with a happily ever after, and men who she claimed have "golden retriever energy but are dominant in the bedroom."

What on earth does that mean? What the hell is golden retriever energy?

There's also a rating she gave each review, including one with a chili pepper, where she discusses… *Oh Emma, you dirty girl.* It's how much sex that's in a book, and it looks like most of her favorites she rates a three or four, out of five.

I shift to get comfortable in bed, having to adjust my too tight pants due to my now very hard dick. She was always so sweet and unassuming in the bedroom when we were together, but was always up for anything. I never pushed her or tested her limits. Maybe that's changed and she's more adventurous?

I scroll more reviews of hers, trying to see what she likes in bed based on her posts, but guilt seeps in. I shouldn't be fantasizing about her like this, when my friend was worried about this very thing. I close out of the app, plug in my phone, and turn out the light on my bedside table.

As I drift off to sleep, I can't help but imagine what it would be like to have her naked in my arms again, her beautiful crystal blue eyes staring back at me with the love she had for me years ago.

Could she be mine again?

Today is the big day. I may have spent the last forty-eight hours overanalyzing everything, even though I'd never admit it out loud. I haven't been on a date in ages and am so incredibly nervous—it doesn't help that it's *Dylan*. No matter how many times I remind myself that we're only catching up, I know in my gut this means more to him.

Dylan said he's taking me to dinner and a movie, but won't give me any details. Riley and Lily agreed to come over to help me decide what to wear. Thankfully, they brought a few bottles of liquid courage.

I apply my makeup in the bathroom, Lily is sipping her glass of Cabernet as she asks, "Okay, so on a scale of one to ten, how likely are you to put out on this date?"

Riley gasps in faux shock. "Come on, Lil, she isn't going to hop into bed with the first guy she dates since Jason. My guess is, if he's as into her now as he was back then, she'll be a solid seven. Better wear the cute panties, Em!"

"Why are you asking me this?" I roll my eyes and fib, "We're getting together as friends! *Just* friends." Dylan may have been the best sex I've ever had, but I am sure as hell not telling them that. It was always the dirty talk that did it for me. Jason let me explore being a little submissive in bed, I wonder if Dylan would...

No, we are just catching up. Nothing more.

Riley takes a sip and replies into her glass, "Em, this is Dylan, the same guy who broke your heart. Sure, Lily and Andrew know him, but that doesn't change the fact that this guy is *not* your friend. There are big feelings there, so stop pretending this is casual. Unless you want it to be? I just don't see you having a one-night stand with him. I have a feeling this guy would wife you up tonight, if you gave him the chance."

She's right; I need to be careful. I turn away from them and examine my reflection in the bathroom mirror as I continue to apply my eye liner, opting for a small wing that's being stubborn. "Fine, so it's *probably* a real date, but I'm not going home with him. I have an early morning tomorrow with my board of directors."

"Keep telling yourself that." Lily cocks an eyebrow at me. "Riley's right, make sure you're wearing your sexiest bra and panties, just in case."

Riley almost spits out her drink laughing. "You should wear them whether you end up naked or not; it'll make you feel confident."

I pull back my hair, ignoring that it's in desperate need of a root touch-up, and tie it in a messy bun—I want to be comfortable in a movie theater and need it high enough that it won't bump against the seat. Taking the girls' advice, I make my way into my room, find my cutest matching bra and panty set, and change into them. They're right; they always are. I feel more confident, even if no one will see them but me. I slip back into my black pencil skirt and a hunter green top that has a high neck but accentuates my curves. It's casual, but formal enough that, if he takes me to a nice restaurant, I won't be under-dressed.

Walking back into the bathroom, Lily is now sitting on the floor, legs crossed, drinking her second glass of wine. Riley is touching up her own makeup. With a deep breath, I twirl and ask them, "Okay, how do I look?"

They both turn to me with huge smiles and twinkling eyes. "Oh, Em, you look amazing!"

Riley pushes past me to my closet and pulls out my one and only pair of Louboutins. "Don't forget the shoes!"

After a couple glasses of red, and way too many positive affirmations in the mirror later, it's already 4:45 p.m. I do a double take at my watch. *How is it already 4:45?*

"Girls, you have to go, he'll be here any minute!"

They scurry to find their purses and shoes, dissolving into a mess of giggles. With a hug and a kiss on the cheek, they are both at my front door, ready to leave. As I open it for them, I find Dylan standing on the other side with his hand poised to knock. Damn it, he's even more attractive than when we dated in our early twenties. It's infuriating that men age so gracefully. In his left hand is a bouquet of violets. My favorite. *He remembered.* Seeing him after all this time has my stomach in knots.

I stumble over my words. "Oh, hey, hi! Sorry, my friends were just leaving." He's staring at me wide-eyed, like I'm a ghost. *Is something wrong with my outfit?* I look down to make sure I look presentable.

When I smooth the front of my skirt, he finally speaks, his voice pulling my gaze back to him. "Wow, E, you look... amazing." He shakes his head, biting his lip. "You haven't changed one bit."

I'm about to reply when Lily shoulders past me to hug Dylan. "Hey, Dylan. Good to see you." She leans in and whispers entirely too loud, probably due to the two glasses of wine, "If you hurt her, I will end you." His eyes widen in response and I can't help but laugh at the fear she's trying to instill in him.

"Hi, we haven't met. I'm Riley."

He takes her hand. "Dylan, nice to meet you."

She eyes him cautiously, then turns to me with a wink. "All right, Em, have a good night!"

As my friends walk away, I hyperfocus on closing the door behind us to hide my growing blush. Key in lock, twist. I'm out of my element here. His hand envelops mine over the handle. It's like static electricity when he touches me—I feel it all the way to my toes. He offers me the bouquet, and says softly, "As much as I can't wait to head out, you might need to put these in water first. I saw them and thought of you. Hope you don't mind the cliché first date etiquette."

I pause, staring at his hand over mine and resisting the shiver running through me. How is it possible that, after all this time, he still makes me feel like this? I glance over his shoulder to make sure my friends are already in their cars, then look back to him—which has to be the worst possible idea. Dylan hasn't lost his adorable dimples when he smiles. "Oh, yeah, sure. Mind coming inside for a moment?"

He nods, still smiling. "Not at all."

Once in the kitchen, I grab a vase from the cabinet next to my fridge and my shears from one of my drawers. I quickly trim the stems to fit my vase and fill it with water. As I turn off the faucet, I finally have the courage to look at him again.

"You know, this isn't technically a first date." I wince. "I'm sorry, this whole thing is weird, right?"

I turn my gaze away quickly. His eyes haven't left me since the moment he walked into my house—I could always feel them on me—and it's making me incredibly nervous.

"I know, but it feels like I missed some milestones the first time. I *did* sort of trick you into dating me." He leans against the counter. Why is leaning so damn sexy?

No, focus. Flowers. Vase.

I let out a small laugh and reply, "True. So, where are we headed?"

"You'll have to wait and see. I recommend pants and not a skirt, though." His eyes darken as they rake over my body. I don't know whether to be afraid or turned on.

I knew there was something off with my outfit!

As I look down at my skirt, I dare to ask, "What's wrong with my skirt? We're going to dinner and you won't tell me where. Will I be overdressed?"

Taking a step toward me, he leans in, his face now mere inches from mine. My breath hitches. "Make no mistake, you are absolutely breathtaking. But if you don't change, I won't be able to keep my hands off you, and I intend on being a gentleman tonight." His voice is low and sultry, making my stomach flip. When he pulls back, I instantly miss him in my space. "Also, we aren't going to a movie, I have something else in mind."

I look at him curiously, his flirting is messing with me. It's been years since I've seen him, but it feels like no time has passed. His words and that damn smile have the same effect on me as they always did. "All right, I'll go change. I'll be back in a few minutes."

I run upstairs and into my room, grateful for the space I put between us. Throwing open my dresser drawers, I take out a pair of skinny jeans. I put them on quickly and text my group chat with Lily and Riley.

> 911!!! He changed plans on me and he won't say what, other than I should wear pants.

RILEY

> Oooh girl, he's sneaky!

LILY

> I just asked Andrew and he said he has no idea. Apparently, he also told Dylan not to date you. I'm sorry I'm no help!

RILEY

> You got this! Magic panties, remember.

I laugh out loud and quickly cover my mouth, nearly forgetting Dylan is right downstairs.

Changed into skinny jeans. Sending you both my location, in case I'm murdered by my ex tonight.

RILEY

Have fun!

LILY

xoxo

I tuck my phone in my back pocket after sharing my location with them. I'm not actually worried, but if they know where I am, they won't be blowing up my phone. After one last look in the mirror, I make my way back downstairs.

"Sorry I took so long. Ready to head out?"

I grab my purse and keys. As I'm about to head to the front door, he reaches for my hand. I consider it for half a second before hesitantly placing my hand in his. It all feels too familiar, especially as he squeezes three times. *I love you.*

My breath catches, remembering what it meant to us when we were together. It doesn't seem to faze him though. *Does he not remember? Or maybe it's just a muscle spasm?*

As soon as we step outside, I make sure to use both hands to lock it. I'm already falling under his spell, just like last time, and need to keep my wits about me—the less physical contact, the better.

We walk the path down the driveway with his hand on the small of my back. Each time he touches me, it feels like déjà vu, and my head swims, unsure if I like the way my feelings are resurfacing.

Okay, fine, I admit it. I like it a bit too much.

8

DYLAN

Emma's absolutely gorgeous, though gorgeous doesn't begin to scratch the surface. I swear she hasn't aged a single day since the last time I saw her. When she opened the door earlier, I was speechless, stunned at how after all this time my heart stops the moment I lay eyes on her. Now that she is in my car next to me, I want to brush my nose against her neck and tuck her close to me. Her perfume is so uniquely her, taking me back to when we were younger. It reminds me of the violets I brought—they were always her favorite.

She's sitting stiffly in her seat, nervously fidgeting with the hem of her shirt. I love and hate that she's nervous. It feels like yesterday we were taking drives down the coast with the wind in our hair for weekend getaways. I've never been able to visit Santa Cruz or Monterey without thinking of her.

I've been reminiscing in silence for far too long. As I pull up to the stop sign at the end of her street, I reach into the backseat and grab a bag for her. "You're going to need this."

Emma eyes me curiously before opening it. I keep one eye on her, waiting for her reaction as I continue driving. She gasps as she pulls out a hoodie from her favorite baseball team—that happen to be playing against my team tonight.

"Hold on, is that where we're going?" She bites her lip, awaiting my response. What I wouldn't give to take that lip between my own teeth.

Not yet, maybe later?

"Yep," I reply as casually as I can. It's Emma, nothing about this is casual. "Is that okay with you?"

"Absolutely!" With the biggest smile I've seen since I arrived at her house, she quickly rips off the tags before putting it on, "Thank you. This is such an amazing surprise."

The drive down the highway to the stadium is torture; the itch to grab her hand in mine is overwhelming. We haven't seen each other in years, it's crazy that I still have such a natural connection with her. Emma fills the silence by telling me about how she thinks this year they will make it to the World Series and how she was supposed to watch the game with her best friend, and is glad she doesn't have to miss it. We used to go to games all the time when we were together, having her here with me feels… *right*.

"How about a wager?"

Raising an eyebrow, she asks, "What kind of wager?"

"If my team wins tonight, I pick where to take you Tuesday. If your team wins, you pick." *Either way, I win.*

She laughs and the cutest crinkles form in the corner of her eyes. "You're relentless! I see that hasn't changed—securing a second date before the first one has even begun. Does that work on all the girls?"

"I don't know. I've only ever tried it on you."

Her breath hitches ever so slightly and she tries to mask it by clearing her throat. "As long as it isn't golf, I'll agree to your terms."

"Oh, come on! You love golf." My reply is dripping with sarcasm and she swats my arm with a laugh. Even the smallest physical contact makes my heart ache. She used to hate golf, I doubt she'll come around to playing eighteen holes with me. Honestly, I couldn't care less what we do, I just want to spend time with her.

I can't help but think about all the lost years that we could've been doing this—the date nights we missed. I should have tried harder to win her back, but I'm not going to let her slip through my fingers this time.

We park, and as I'm about to exit the car, her hand covers mine. "Dylan, thank you, truly. This is so unexpected and thoughtful."

I turn my hand and interlace our fingers, squeezing three times—a reminder that I still love her. Her pupils dilate; she remembers. "Thank you for coming, E."

We smile at each other for a moment before I step out and circle the car for her to do the same. I've never let her open her own door and she stopped fighting me about a week into dating when we were younger. Yet another thing I've missed.

The biggest surprise of the night is our seats are directly behind home plate. I owe a buddy at work at least four thousand favors for giving me his season seats for the night, with less than a day's notice. Before we make our way to our section, I offer, "We're still a little early, want to grab a drink or a bite to eat?"

"Sure, lead the way," Emma beams with a smile that could light up the whole stadium. Definitely worth the four thousand favors.

I use the opportunity to hold her hand again, but every time I touch her, my chest tightens. I've never missed someone who is standing right in front of me before. Unable to help myself, I steal glances as we walk and guide her to the small sports bar near our section. She's still so beautiful, it hurts to take my eyes off her for even a moment.

It's fairly busy but we manage to find a small table. I pull her seat out for her and as I push it in I'm met with the familiar scent of violets. This close to her, I'm struggling to resist the urge to kiss her bare neck.

"Usual, E?"

Her spine straightens, and I swear she lets out a soft moan. She turns to look at me, our faces close enough that if I moved just an inch...

"Yes, mine with extra lime, please." Emma's cheeks are dusted light pink as turns away from me quickly. I love that I can still make her blush. She's tougher than steel but has always melted for me. Little does she know that one little word leaves another ache in my chest: *Mine*.

The bartender spots me approaching and asks, "What'll it be?"

"Two gin and tonics, one with extra lime, please." I hand him my card, leaving the tab open. He nods and makes our drinks. As I take them back to our table, I set one in front of Emma. She's on her phone, smiling. "Anyone I know?"

Emma looks up, embarrassed. "Oh, no, just a friend sent me a funny meme." She quickly pockets her phone, but I can't help the jealousy that hits me. *Was it guy friend? Someone she's seeing.* As if reading my thoughts, she explains, "My best friend, actually, since college. I tagged my location on social media. When they saw I was here, I was sent a funny meme about how my team will beat yours. I'll have to introduce you sometime! They moved away after college, before you and I..." She doesn't complete her thought, instead reaching to pick up her drink and bringing it to her lips for a few sips. Her eyes never leave mine, even as she sets it down. "Thank you, again, this is all so amazing! I haven't been to a game in forever." I want to address what she was going to say, but decide to leave it be... for now.

After two rounds of drinks, we've talked about current work projects, our kids, and basic surface-level conversation catching up. I already know most of it from my internet deep-dive the other night, but I love that she's sharing with me all the same. "So, still planning on taking over the world?"

"Of course! Well, maybe not the whole world. I do have big plans, though. I'm hoping to become President at the agency by the end of the year. It'll be a lot of work but it's my dream—I know I can take the company to the next level."

I love that she still has ambitious goals and I find myself wanting to be part of them. I plant the seed. "Will that leave time for… other things in your life?"

"As in?" A small smirk tugs at the corner of her lips as she sips her drink.

"Oh, I don't know, maybe dating someone who you haven't seen in years, but has always been yours?"

Her eyes widen and she sucks in a breath. "That's a *very* specific question."

"That it is." I slowly bring my drink to my lips, admiring the beautiful crimson dusting her cheeks, and I can't wipe the smile off my face.

I glance up at the TV behind her; the game is already the top of the third. She follows my line of sight. "Oh shoot, the game started! We must have lost track of time. Should we find our seats?"

I would be more than happy sitting here talking with her all night, but I take our now empty glasses to the bar, and close our tab. As we leave, I guide her by the small of her back to our seats.

Two innings later, I've been so distracted by her that I don't even know what the score is. While I'm typically competitive when it comes to the game, I couldn't care less. She's here with me, after all this time.

"What sounds good for dinner?"

Emma taps her finger to her lips and hums as she ponders. "How about a few hotdogs when the vendor comes by? And if your team is magically up at the bottom of the inning, dinner is on me."

I let out a small laugh as I check the score. "Not exactly fair given how many runs my team needs to catch up, but you have a deal."

There is no way in hell I'm letting her pay, and she knows it.

9

EMMA

I feel a *little* bad. My team is up nine to one, and it's only the bottom of the sixth. We've been laughing, yelling at players who can't hear us, and I'm truly having an amazing time. It's almost too easy… *Except for that question he asked me at the bar.*

There's always been something about Dylan; he has an energy that everyone is drawn to. It was one of the things I loved about him when we first started dating, but as things got serious between us, it started to destroy my self esteem. The fact that he was more attractive and outgoing than me had me constantly worry I wasn't good enough—even if it was all in my head.

With the seventh inning stretch upon us, I get up to grab us a couple beers. I'm halfway out of my seat when he playfully grabs my wrist. "Hey, where do you think you're going?"

"Oh, I was just going to get us a few drinks."

His grip tightens slightly and he tugs me down toward him until our faces are inches apart. My whole body is tingling; he so easily possesses me, only holding my wrist. I can't help wondering what would happen if I went home with him tonight.

Man, I need to walk this off!

It's been a while since I've had sex, but it's ridiculous how turned on I am at the thought of surrendering to him in bed.

Where just a few moments ago he was sporting an ear to ear grin, he's now frowning. "If you think, for one moment, that I'm going to let you buy drinks for us, you've lost your mind. I know you always hated it when I doted on you, but tonight you're going to let me." His expression softens, but his gaze is still lethal. "We have drink service with our seats. I've got this." His voice lowers to just above a whisper and in silkiest voice I have ever heard, asks, "Are you going to be my good girl and let me take care of you?"

Dylan presses a kiss to the inside of my wrist, making my body buzz with arousal. I swallow hard and I sit back down. He waves down one of the servers, then rests his arm behind my chair. I'm frozen in my seat, trying to process what he just said. *Does he know calling me that is a total turn on for me?* Everything since we've reconnected is as if he's read all of my favorite books and conjured up the ulti- mate book boyfriend to play for the night.

Before the server makes their way to us, I hear a dreaded announcement over the speakers. "All right, everyone! It's time to pucker up! It's Kiss Cam time!"

Fuck. Fuck, fuck, fuck. Please, for the love, don't pan to us!

I absolutely want to kiss him, especially after that little interaction, but I sure as hell don't want it to be because of a damn kiss cam. As if he can sense my discomfort, he stands and offers his hand. "Come on, let's get up and stretch our legs. We can grab drinks at the bar, instead."

We take a walk around the stadium, holding hands; I definitely needed to move after sitting for so long. We wander to the end of right field. I assume we'll return the way we came and grab a beer, but he pauses, stopping us in our tracks. His gaze falls to my lips, then back to my eyes.

"E, since the moment I saw you tonight, I've wanted to kiss you." He looks out toward the stadium, and continues, "While I wouldn't mind it being in front of hundreds of people, the way I want to kiss you is not at all appropriate for a jumbotron." He snakes his hand to my lower back, pulling me close until my chest is flush against his. My body hums in anticipation as I place my palms on his chest to brace myself.

"And how do you want to kiss me, Mr. Alexander?"

I knew damn well what I was getting myself into as soon as those words left my lips. A rumble echoes in his chest, vibrating beneath my fingertips. He doesn't respond with words, instead, backing me up until I feel the railing behind me. The movement steals my breath from me, and I almost stumble. I immediately regret wearing heels tonight, no matter how sexy they make my legs look. He releases my hand, both of his now cupping my face, pulling my lips to his.

Our second, first kiss starts slow, almost innocent, taking me back to when we were younger. I'm secretly hoping he will take this further, like he promised. I know I'm playing with fire but I can't help the moan that escapes me as he licks the seam of my lips.

"*Emma*," he growls into my mouth; a warning, one I should heed.

I do no such thing, instead lightly nipping his lower lip as I pull away from him. "Hmm?" I purr back.

As if I unleashed a caged wild animal, his mouth crashes into mine. None of it is gentle; it's commanding, as if he's trying to make up for lost time in one kiss. Years of pent up anger and hurt melt away as his tongue sweeps across mine. Someone clears their throat behind him, causing us to abruptly end what could have easily been one of the best kisses of my life. I let out a whimper as his lips leave mine. The man was trying to devour me and it clearly did something for him, based on his hard length pressed against me.

I'm still sandwiched between him and the railing when I attempt to collect myself. "*Dylan.*" My voice comes out like a plea, even if I didn't intend it. "We, uh… we should get back to our seats." He kisses me on the cheek, barely a peck, then steps away from me without a word. He slips his hand into mine as we walk back to our section as if nothing happened. I can barely walk after that panty-melting kiss, how is he so collected? *Great, now I'm thinking about my panties, and how I'll probably need to ditch them soon.* My whole body is on fire from one kiss.

So much for being "just friends."

It's a boring last few innings of the game, except that he hasn't let go of my hand the entire time. It's comfortable, a little *too* comfortable, for a first date. It makes me nervous all over again. That kiss… I don't remember him having so much passion and he definitely never called me a "good girl" before. He's the same man, but different in so many ways.

The final score is twelve to two. Yes, I'm a sore winner, and may have celebrated a little too loudly. Dylan doesn't seem to mind; he already knows that about me. Standing first, he offers his hand to pull me to my feet. It's a little too hard and fast and I end up chest to chest with him. He wraps an arm around my back to steady me, keeping me close, his hungry eyes falling to my lips. *Is he going to kiss me again?*

I begin to question the state of my lipstick—which claims to be smudge-proof and kiss-proof. After a hotdog, that heady makeout session at right field, and a few drinks, I'm not so sure. He doesn't lean in, making it feel like a stand-off. The electricity between us is unmistakable. It was intense when we were together before, but this is a whole other level. He enjoys taking control, and I want him to take what's his.

Seriously? One kiss and I'm a damn Dylan stan?

To my disappointment, he releases me and takes half a step back. I clear my throat, "Ready to make out? Crap. I, uh, mean head out. Ready to head out?"

Oh. My. God. I did not just say that!

"Yeah." He lets out a low chuckle that makes my belly flip and I'm left dumbfounded, unsure which question he's answering. He takes my hand and leads us up the steps—I guess there's my answer. Probably for the best. I don't like how I slipped into routine with him so easily. My head and heart say we need to take this slow, but my body is protesting *very* loudly.

I stop him for a moment before we exit. "Mind if I use the restroom first?"

"Of course not. Take your time." He reluctantly releases my hand, squeezing it three times before letting go. The old habit of his has to be a tick. *Unless... Is it possible? No.* "I'll be over at the cart grabbing a couple of water bottles for the road."

I rush to the bathroom; my bladder is about to explode. I didn't want to be *that girl* who gets up during a game, but now I'm regretting it. Also, I definitely need to get rid of these panties. It's becoming quite uncomfortable with all the sexual tension between us. It was one kiss, and I'm not just wet, I'm freaking soaked. My damn body is betraying me tonight, my vibrator will absolutely be put to work later tonight.

Once I'm done, I wash and dry my hands. When I look in the mirror, I'm impressed that my lipstick is still immaculate. I pull my hair out of the bun and debate whether to leave it. He always loved it when I wore my hair down, and I'm feeling a little flirty right now. I comb my fingers through my faux auburn locks, impressed that it's not a rat's nest for the first time in ages—there's a bit of a beach wave from being up most of the day. I touch up my lipstick and with a final 'fit check, I head out to find Dylan.

I walk toward the cart Dylan said he would be at, but he's nowhere to be found. I look around, and for a brief moment nearly panic that he left me here.

No, he wouldn't do that. We're at a game, this isn't sixteen years ago when he ghosted you.

As I'm about to pull out my phone, I spot him leaning against a pillar a few aisles down from where I'm at, two water bottles in one hand and checking his phone in the other. He glances up, and when his eyes meet mine, he lights up. Pushing off the pillar and pocketing his phone, he begins walking toward me like a lion on the prowl. The closer he gets, the more heat is visible in his eyes. I hold out my hand for him to take it, but he quickly wraps his arm around to my lower back, pulling me in close like earlier.

He knocks the breath out of me and I tease, "Whoa there, tiger! You forgot I'm wearing heels, I nearly fell over."

"What did you expect?" The same growl from before settles in his chest. "You're an absolute goddess, E. How could I keep my hands to myself?"

I place my hands to his chest and look up at him with doe eyes. "*Mr. Alexander*, you're such a flirt! Are you ready to go?" I know the risks of flirting with him like this; I've slipped back into the Emma I was when I was with him. It's reckless and should tone it down, before one of us takes things too far.

He shakes his head with a chuckle. "No, Emma, I am not ready to let you go."

I'm at a loss for words. Surely he couldn't mean it the way he said it. Still, I need to keep it light. With a bright smile, I reply, "Okay, but the stadium is emptying out, we can't stay here forever." I open my bag and gesture for him to put the water bottles in.

I expect him to release me, but he leans in to delicately kiss my cheek, then presses his own cheek against mine. His hot breath fans my ear as he whispers, "No, but if I had my way, I'd keep you forever."

He pulls back, searching for the green light to kiss me. My mind reeling a million miles a minute, but my body has a mind of its own. I press a chaste kiss to his lips and pull away as quickly. I don't trust myself right now, and if we don't get out of here soon, I'm afraid I'll climb him like a tree, banned from ever attending a baseball game again. I attempt to retreat from him so we can leave, but he holds me in place.

Dylan presses his forehead to mine with a sigh. "I am so sorry I ever let you go." He pulls back with sad eyes. As he steps back and offers his hand, I miss his warmth. "Shall we?"

I blow out a long breath that comes out as a sigh. "Yeah, I need to get home… early morning meetings."

All traces of his consistent smile have faded. I take his hand and we walk back to his car. I overthink everything, but the change in energy between us is no longer playful and light. I can't handle the dark cloud looming over us. I hate it.

The car ride home is nearly silent, with only the music on the radio filling the void. It's only twenty minutes to my house, but feels like eternity. When we arrive, he turns off the engine, steps out of the car, and circles it to open my door. I know the routine. He never let me open doors back then, I doubt he would let me now. I step out and we walk to my front door.

With my head down, fiddling with my keys, I don't know what we are doing but I am not liking the shift between us since we left the game. Maybe this whole thing was a mistake?

"Thank you for tonight, I had an amazing time." I lift my gaze. There's a swirl of emotion in his eyes—a little lust, a dash of sadness, and a whole lot of disappointment. He tilts my chin a little higher. I can't look away, even if the searing eye contact transports me back in time, making me feel like I'm twenty-one all over again.

He pauses for a moment and asks with so much worry in his voice, "Did I… Did I mess everything up? Moving too fast tonight? Because I need to be honest, Emma, I never stopped loving you. I need to know if I have a shot at making you mine again."

Before I can respond, Dylan tucks a few strands of my hair behind my ear. Instead of pulling away, he wraps his fingers around the back of my neck to pull me a few inches closer. His eyes dart between mine, as if to ask permission. I give in, nodding ever so slightly and waiting for him to make the final move. Without wasting another moment, his mouth crushes mine. This isn't the Dylan I knew when we were younger. He is kissing me like I might disappear if he stops.

His hand wanders from the back of my neck to the front of my throat, as he continues to claim my mouth. It feels too familiar, him owning me like this. *It's too much.* I tear my lips away from him, wrap both of my arms around his back, and press my forehead against his chiseled pecs. *When did he get so ripped?* "I'm sorry. As much as I want you to come in, I can't do this. It's… it's too soon."

He kisses the top of my head and whispers into my hair, "Don't apologize, it's okay, E. I didn't expect to come in. I'm sorry if I took things too far. Honestly, I would wait a thousand years, if it meant I could hold you in my arms like this again."

"You can't say things like that, not after…" I can't say it out loud; the pain floods through me. Tears prick behind my eyes and all the fears I suppressed tonight come rushing to the surface. I was so in love with him, and I wasn't sure I'd ever love anyone the same way. He broke me and it took so long to pick up the pieces. While the last few hours erased *some* of the last decade or two, it's still too fast. "You know it's hard to say no to you, especially when you kiss me like that." I take a deep breath before I continue, "You've been very clear about your intentions, and I'm… I'm just not ready to fall in love with you again. I know that's *exactly* what would happen if we don't slow down."

I glance up, finding his eyes full of hope. With a soft smile, he presses a single kiss to my forehead. "Would that be so bad? Falling in love with me again? I know I messed things up when we were younger. But we're different people now. One day with you and I know whatever this is, it's imminent. We've always moved fast, but I promise if you give us a shot, I'll never hurt you again."

I can't do this. Not with him, With a deep breath, I tell him the only logical thing that comes to mind, "You can't promise me that," shaking my head and attempt to break the eye contact he demands.

"Yes, I absolutely can. This, you and me, we were always meant to be together. All I'm asking for is a chance to prove it to you. One chance. Sure, I would be lying if I said I haven't thought about you naked in my bed, but it's more than that. It's like a piece of my heart was missing, and being with you tonight, it feels whole again." He pulls away, takes my hand, bringing my palm to his lips for a soft kiss. "Please, Emma. We can take this as slow as you want."

I'll likely regret it, but what if he's right? I reach to brush a stray lock of hair off his forehead, and he closes his eyes as he leans into my touch. Against my better judgment, I give him the answer he seeks, "Okay. Slow." My favorite dimples appear and I can't help smiling back at him.

I step back as he bends to pick up my keys I dropped during this emotional rollercoaster. I unlock the door, step inside, and turn back to say goodnight before closing it. Once the door clicks, I lean my back against the door to collect myself.

As I'm about to pull out my phone to call Riley, there's a soft knock behind me. Knowing it's him, I open the door without checking the peephole. Dylan's hunched forward, bracing himself on each side of the door frame. As I open it further, he looks up, his eyes full of desperation. "Can I stay the night?"

I quirk an eyebrow at him and cross my arms over my chest. "*Really?* What happened to taking things slow?"

He bites his lip and chuckles softly. "The girls are with my parents tonight. I'm afraid that if I leave you right now, you'll second guess all of this, and I won't see you again for another few decades." I'm not convinced, keeping my expression neutral, as he continues, "I'll be on my best behavior. A perfect gentleman, I promise. I'm just not ready to say goodnight... And I don't think you are either."

Should I say yes? Probably not. But my lady bits are calling the shots tonight, so with a deep breath, I gesture inside with my head anyway. "Come on, I'll put on the kettle."

All sadness in his expression is replaced with lust he's trying to keep contained. It's definitely a mistake. A smart woman would send him away. After he walks in, I close the door behind him, second guessing my decision. While I don't have the boys tonight, having the only man I've ever loved in my house is a terrible idea. I set the door alarm for the night, put my phone in my back pocket, and follow him into the kitchen. It's unlikely he'll be the gentleman he claims to be, and won't be able to keep his hands to himself. Worse, I'm not entirely sure I want him to.

I kick off my heels beside the kitchen island; as sexy as they are, my feet are incredibly sore from the long evening. Pulling two mugs out of the cabinet, I place them on the counter in front of me and scan the next cabinet before asking, "Peppermint, green, or chamomile?"

Dylan comes up behind me to examine my tea options—I have twenty-three, but he wouldn't know what half of them are. He reaches above my head to grab the box of lavender earl grey tea and sets it on the counter. It's my favorite, but there's no way he could know that.

Instead of pulling his hand back, he cages me in on both sides, his chest against my back and… *Oh.* How is it possible that he's hard without me even touching him? Part of me wants to unzip his pants, drop to my knees, and take him in my mouth right here, just to hear him call me a good girl again. *Whoa, where did that thought come from?* I need to lay off the mafia romance books for a while. Having him so close is making me throw all logic out the window.

"I'm sorry, you just look so good in these jeans." He splays his hand across my stomach, and pulls me impossibly closer to him. It may have been years, but he still remembers how to disarm me. His lips travel from my ear to my neck, kissing me softly. "Is this okay?"

Trying my hardest to keep my composure, I clear my throat and will my pussy to calm the hell down. "You, um, you said you would be on your best behavior. This is *not* that. Sounds like my pants are the problem. I'll run upstairs and change. Mind starting the water?"

Gently nipping at my earlobe before letting me go, he purrs, "Not at all, beautiful." All of the air in my lungs is gone, so I do the most sensible thing I can—turn away from him and rush toward the stairs as quickly as I can manage.

I take them two at a time and power walk into my bedroom. Once inside, I pace for a moment. *What was that? How can he have this kind of effect on me after just a few hours?* It felt so good to have him touch me, but I need to stop this. Right now. I open my dresser to look for the least sexy pants I have and a comfy shirt. I settle on a pair of white and black buffalo plaid drawstring pajama pants that Lily, Riley, and I wear when we're doing a romance movie marathon, and a plain black t-shirt. I also grab underwear, since my last pair was trashed after having his mouth and hands on me at the game. I quickly change and make sure to grab my phone from my jeans. After putting my hoodie back on, I make my way back downstairs, glad to have as much clothing between us as humanly possible.

As I approach the kitchen, there's a whistle of the kettle before he turns the burner off. I bring the prepped mugs over and set them next to the stove.

"Hey, I couldn't find your sugar, but it looks like I found something even more delicious."

With one quick motion, he lifts me by my waist, and I let out a little squeak as he sets me on my island, opposite the stove. "Dylan, what are you doing? Come on, does that line actually work on anyone?"

We're now almost the same height, which is convenient but problematic if we are trying to take things slow. He steps between my legs. *Nope, it's definitely problematic.*

"What does it look like I'm doing, E? And you tell me, did it work on you?"

"Hey!" I playfully swat at his chest. "You said you would be a perfect gentleman, and I would hardly consider you a Mr. Darcy right now."

"Perhaps you're right. Around you, I am more of a Wickham."

I gasp in fake horror, clutching a hand to my chest. "Why, good sir, what are your intentions then? Wait a second… since when do you know Jane Austen characters?"

"Are you serious? Did you forget? You made me watch the movies with you, I have them practically memorized." He places his hands on my thighs, stroking casual circles with his thumbs, and I do my best to stifle a moan. "But, to answer your first question, I intended to come in here, keep my hands to myself, and if you let me, I'd spend an unforgettable night with you in my arms." His eyes darken as he continues, "But now? Now, I'm fighting the urge to lift you off this counter, carry you upstairs, and worship every inch of your body until I have branded you as mine again."

"Dylan," I breathe. I'm so turned on, but we just talked about why we can't do this. "I—"

He puts his finger to my lips for a brief moment to quiet me, then rests his forehead on mine again. "No, E, I'm sorry, I shouldn't have said that. While I have dreamt about my face between your legs all night, you're right. I promised I would be a perfect gentleman if you invited me in. I want you to trust me again, and I know you're not ready for us yet. So, as much as I want to, I won't touch you... *tonight*."

_____

10

EMMA

I wake up wrapped in Dylan's arms, a strangely familiar feeling. He held me against him all night, as if these past sixteen years never existed.

What are you doing? Why did you let him into your house? You've lost your damn mind! Screw letting him in the house, why the hell did you let him stay the night? He's going to hurt you again!

I need to put an end to it. Well… maybe after I enjoy a few more minutes.

"Don't overthink this, Emma," Dylan murmurs into my neck with a light chuckle that vibrates through me. He presses soft kisses on my shoulder and moves his hand to hold mine, only furthering my mind's tug-of-war. "I meant it when I said we'll take this slow—as slow as you want." He pulls me closer. "I know I kind of love-bombed you last night, but I don't regret asking to stay. I didn't realize how much I missed waking up with you."

I turn to face him. He lets go of my hand to wrap his arm around my back, tracing lazy circles along my spine that light me up inside. "It's just a lot. We haven't talked in years, and yet, here you are in my bed as if the last few decades never happened. What are we doing? I thought we were taking this slow."

My concern brings a smile to his face, which should alarm me, but doesn't. Damn hormones. "I can think of a few slow things I would like to do to you right now." He wiggles his eyebrows and I playfully pat his chest in response.

"You're impossible!" I'm grateful for his playfulness, though. I'm not sure how much of his emotional declarations I can handle.

The romance refuses to cease as he kisses my temple and tucks my hair behind my ear. "I'm kidding, E. Well, mostly. I promise, I'm actually trying my best to take things slow with you. It's just new for us." He laughs to himself, shaking his head. "You know, I remember the first time I saw you standing across that room, calling to me like a fucking siren. I couldn't take my eyes off you, couldn't stay away from you. I still can't. I know you feel it too. You can fight it all you want, and we can *try* to take this slow, but you and I both know where this is headed. I'm all in, Emma. So, I'll wait for you to catch up."

My heart is screaming "*yes*," but my head refuses to join in. "I can't just jump into a relationship. I have kids. *You* have kids. We need to be smart about this, and you staying over was *not* smart."

"I know you, but I knew if I left last night, I would drive home alone and you would talk yourself out of this. I couldn't risk it." His eyes hold so much agony in them, like a sad puppy looking for a home. He wants to pick up where we left off so many years ago, but I'm not sure that I'm ready for that.

I sigh. "What if I can't do this?"

My words hurt him, but he purses his lips and nods, his hand traveling from my back, up my arm, all the way to my chin, holding it in place. "Then, at least, I got one night. One night I could pretend you were mine again. But I'm not going anywhere. I meant what I said: I'll wait for you to catch up."

Dylan closes the distance to kiss me, and as his lips almost reach mine, my alarm startles us both, killing the moment. He laughs and I feel it everywhere. Breaking the silence, he casually announces, "Well, I guess that's my cue," then presses his lips to mine for just a moment—a ghost of a kiss. After releasing me from his embrace, he shifts off the bed, and turns off the alarm. He went to bed wearing just his shirt and boxer briefs. I'm not a monster, I wasn't going to make him wear jeans to bed. With his back to me, he slips on his pants and I can't help but stare.

Damn, he's hot. When did back muscles become such a turn on for me?

I move off the bed, padding off to the bathroom to get ready for work. As I reach the door of my ensuite, he asks, "Mind if I grab a cup of coffee before I leave?"

I stop in my tracks and turn around. "Oh, uh, sure, of course. I need about twenty minutes to get ready. If you need to leave, the code for the alarm is zero, two, one, four to disarm it before you open the door." I really hope he doesn't pick up on the significance of my alarm code.

His smile wide, he replies, "I don't have any meetings 'til ten. I'll wait for you." Shaking his head and muttering to himself, he leaves my bedroom and I rush to the bathroom to turn on the shower.

I take the fastest shower of my life, put my hair up in a neat bun using a hair accessory that looks like a slap bracelet I had as a kid, then quickly apply foundation, mascara, and my favorite red lipstick. I throw on a flowy ivory button-up blouse and my navy blazer with a matching pencil skirt. After getting dressed in record time, I pick out a pair of ballet flats and my sky high stilettos that match my top. I'm a practical woman; those heels are only going on when absolutely necessary. With my shoes in hand, I leave my bedroom and trot downstairs, welcomed by the smell of coffee.

Dylan is leaning against the counter by the coffee maker, phone in one hand—either reading or scrolling—and coffee in the other. *Oof, the lean, again.* He looks up from his phone as I enter the kitchen.

"Wow, you look… I have no words, E." He then mutters under his breath, "Andrew was right. So out of my league." I don't think I was supposed to hear that bit, but he doesn't seem to care. I glance down at my clothes; I'm not wearing anything special, but he makes me feel like I am. "I made a whole pot so you could have one cup with me and have enough to take one to-go."

Why does he have to be so thoughtful? I'm in trouble.

I thank him as I grab my oat milk creamer from the fridge and pour myself a cup. We sip our coffees in comfortable silence for a moment, but it's interrupted by my phone buzzing on the counter with a text from my assistant.

PHOEBE

Good morning! Not sure if you saw the calendar update, but I wanted to let you know that your 8 a.m. meeting was moved to 2:45 p.m.

I consider the message for a minute. If I stay here for another moment in my kitchen—with this man who fits entirely too well in it—I'll march his sexy ass upstairs and won't leave for a month.

I need to get out of here!

My gaze lifts to Dylan and I lie, "Looks like one of my meetings was moved up. Are you ready to go?"

Without a rebuttal, he takes my mug from me. His fingers barely touching mine but still send a chill all over my body. He sets our mugs in the sink and fills my travel mug. I watch him intently as he opens my fridge to pull out my creamer and adds the *perfect* amount to the coffee. After returning it, he hands me my coffee. Taking my free hand, he gestures to the door. "Now I am."

Ugh, why is he so smooth?

I pull my hand back to grab my phone, keys, and purse, looking for any reason to keep my hands full and out of his. The jerk knows what I'm doing, a small smirk tugging on his lips as he takes my cup to carry it so we can interlace our fingers again.

Dylan leads the way to my front door, releasing our joined hands long enough to disarm and open it. "Valentine's Day, huh?"

"What?"

"Your code, E."

Crap, he figured it out.

"Oh, yeah, I guess it is." I hope my non-answer satisfies his curiosity. His knowing smirk says otherwise.

Dylan takes out his phone and hands it to me. "Unlock it." I frown in confusion. "Zero-two-one-four."

No matter how hard I try to hide my surprise, I can't, and don't unlock it. "Quite the coincidence."

"Quite," he replies, typing the numbers once to prove it'll unlock, then tucks it back in his pocket.

Once I lock up, I turn back to him waiting for me less than a foot away. I'm confident he won't let me out of his sight until I drive off.

We walk in amenable silence to my car parked next to his in my driveway. I unlock it and he opens the driver's side for me. Before I get in, he lifts my knuckles to his lips for a quick kiss; his eyes never leave mine.

"Have a great day at work, beautiful."

I smile back at him. How could I not? "You too." He releases my hand for me to slide into my seat, and I set everything down as he closes my car door. Looking out the window, I start my car and he steps back a few feet. All I can do is give him an awkward small wave as I leave.

The drive to the office is too quiet. I don't want to be alone with my thoughts, so I open my audiobook app, but remember I never called Riley last night, as promised. I would call Lily, but she's a hopeless romantic, and will probably start planning our wedding if I tell her what happened. Riley is the logical, practical one; I need her to help me keep my head on straight. I press my hands-free button on my car, and command: "Call Riley."

She picks up on the second ring. "Spill, tell me *everything!*"

"Good morning to you, too! There isn't much to tell," I fib. It isn't as if I could tell her how much of a mistake it was to go out with Dylan, then invite him to stay over. Except, the truth always comes out.

"You are so full of crap! You would've called me last night for a date debrief, but instead I didn't hear from you until now? I'm not buying it. So, what really happened?" She gasps. "You slept with him, didn't you?"

"No! I mean, sure, part of me wanted to, but we agreed to take it slow."

I continue to debrief her on my date. She stays silent for most of my story and I even dare to tell her how he asked to stay over, admitting we spent the night together. He kept his promise, nothing happened.

Except, it did feel amazing waking up in his arms.

"Let me get this straight… He poured his heart out to you, like some kind of confession you'd expect from a book boyfriend written by one of those romance authors you represent. Then, he admitted—more than once—that he never stopped loving you? What did you say?"

It hits me. I didn't reciprocate his feelings. "Um, I don't remember exactly, but I didn't tell him I love him back."

"Do you, though?"

I think about her question, shifting in my seat. "I, uh… No. I haven't loved him since he broke my heart." It's the truth, I'm not there.

She sighs. "That's what I thought. It was probably nice having a hot man in your bed. I understand wanting a doting, growly, alpha-type meandering around your house for the night, ready to pin you against the wall at any given moment. Did he call you a good girl? I bet he did, he seems the type. Anyway, I'm getting off track… Okay, I hope you know I say this with love; please hear me out. You are so freaking stubborn when it comes to forgiveness." I almost object, but she continues, "Don't lead him on if you aren't ready to be serious with him. I know he said *I'll wait forever for you*, or whatever line he pulled that sounded all fluffy and cozy, but here's the reality: You are a strong, independent woman, who runs one of the largest agencies in the US. Don't forget what a badass you are! Of course, you're the one who got away! Don't let one night cloud your judgment by thinking this guy is endgame. Sure, it's possible he might be, but let's not get ahead of ourselves. He promised to take it slow, so take it slow."

This is why I adore Riley; she always keeps me grounded and why I didn't call Lily. "You're right. So, we made plans for tomorrow night, but I think I need to cancel." I chew on my lip and add, "It's too much, too soon."

"You're call, hun. If you want my opinion, I think it's smart to take some time and let the emotions settle. Maybe move it out a week? If he starts texting you some flirty shit that gets you feeling all hot and bothered, put your phone on 'do not disturb,' take a deep breath, and remind yourself that you've only been talking to this guy for a few days. You don't know him, and he doesn't know you. Give yourselves time to get to know each other again. In a week, if you still want to date him, then go for it. If it's going to work with him, you need time, Em."

I sigh. "Why do you always know exactly what to say?"

"Well, I am older and wiser."

"By, like, three months! I'm going to postpone the date a week, it will give me time to cool off." I make a mental note to cancel my sitter. I do want to date him, but I need a little space to process everything first.

She laughs. "Okay, since that's settled, let's make it a girls night tomorrow. That way you aren't moping around, wishing you'd been on a date with him."

"Sounds good, I'll text Lily to see if she's free."

"Buffalo plaid?"

I smile at the thought of our pajama get-togethers we have when one of us had a rough day or is celebrating. Only, I wish it was the latter. I confirm, "I'm in. It's definitely going to be a buffalo plaid night."

We hang up as I'm pulling into my parking spot at work. I text Lily and Riley.

> Tomorrow night. Buffalo plaid?

LILY

Oh no! Did the date not go well?

> It went too well. I'll explain tomorrow over a bottle of wine, pizza, and Pride and Prejudice... You know which one.

LILY

If we're watching Colin Firth, instead of our usual movie where they need to save the small town hot chocolate shop and fall in love, it must be bad.

Bad? Not exactly, I just need some girlfriend time to wrap my head around the whole thing. See you then?

RILEY

I'm in, I'll bring dessert.

LILY

I'll bring the wine!

11

DYLAN

After staying at Emma's last night, I'll admit, I'm a bit overconfident things are on the right track.

When I get in the building, there is an undeniable pep in my step. It's a typical Monday morning, except it means I get to see Emma tomorrow. As I greet all of my favorite people, you can almost hear Dean Martin crooning in the background like a damn movie montage. I settle into my usual routine of emails and meetings. About an hour into my day, my phone vibrates in my pocket.

> EMMA
>
> Thank you so much for last night! My sitter bailed on me for Tuesday. Sorry, I won't be able to make it.

I pause, contemplating my response; I should wait until later today to respond. *Wait, does my phone send read receipts?* Fuck, it does. I don't want her to think I'm ignoring her, or that this is anything like last time, so I type out a reply.

> Raincheck? How about Friday?

She's out sick for the week.

Maybe this weekend?

I promised my boys it would be a family weekend.

So much for being on the right track.

When's the next time you're free?

After several agonizing minutes, she finally responds.

Maybe next week? Can I let you know?

I purposefully don't open our conversation again. I saw enough of the message to know what it says without her knowing I read it. I have no idea how to respond to that, and I wish I knew what changed in the last few hours. I agreed to take things slow, at her pace, but this sounds more like a brush off.

Pulling up my call log, I click on Andrew's name, but after four rings, it goes to voicemail. Twenty agonizing minutes later, he calls me back and I pick up, hoping any anxious thoughts I had aren't apparent in my tone. "Hey, Drew, how's it going?"

"Oh, you know, it's going. Typical Monday shit. Sorry I missed your call. What's up?" He sounds distracted.

"So, I went out with Emma last night." I pause for a response, but am met with silence on the other end, so I continue, "It went great. I took her to a game, and we spent an incredible night together." I pause a second time, but he's still quiet. "So, anyway, this morning she canceled our Tuesday plans."

"Did I call it? Or did I call it? He sighs. "I'm sorry, I have no idea what's going on. Lily said she's going to Emma's tomorrow, something about a Jane Austen emergency. What did Emma say exactly?"

"That her sitter canceled."

"Well, I mean, it's possible she's telling the truth. Their pajama night is at her house. Maybe she was just bummed that she had to cancel and invited her friends over? I don't know, it's weird talking to you about this." Frustration seeps into every one of his words. "It's why I didn't want you to date my wife's best friend!"

"I know. I know," I sigh. "It was just a *perfect night* and an amazing morning." Realizing my slip-up and quickly correct myself. "I mean, our texts this morning."

"Fuck. Did you sleep with her?"

I wince. "I mean, technically, yes, but we just *slept*. I told her I would take things at her pace. We're going to take things slow." Except slow for me is a bullet train.

"News flash! Emma is *not* a casual girl. I told you this! The fact that you stayed over at all, she's probably freaking out. You moved too fast." He clarifies, "Okay, you remember Jeff, my old boss?"

"Yeah, what does that have to do with this?" I shudder. Jeff was a human version of a Palm Pilot.

"Well, that's Emma. Except, she's pretty and makes amazing pumpkin bread."

"I'm not following. That doesn't sound like the Emma I know." Sure, the Emma I know is an overthinker, but when we are together there is so much passion and… *love.* Deep down she still loves me, but she's fighting it. I know we've been apart for a long time, but there's no way she changed that much. Yesterday, it felt like we picked up where we left off.

"Emma is the most organized and professional, *but cynical,* woman I've ever known. She schedules every minute of every day, she has to. But"—he pauses for dramatic effect—"worst of all, she holds one hell of a grudge. It's why she's so good at her job. She establishes strong working relationships, and lets go of vendors and authors who break their contracts. Emma doesn't do second chances. As soon as I figured out that you were the one who broke her heart all those years ago, I knew you were screwed."

Am I screwed? Will she ever forgive me? "No, that's all in the past. We had an amazing night—"

He interrupts, "Where she texts you the next day, bails on you, and is now hanging out with my wife instead?"

"So, what do I do? I don't want to mess this up." The more I think about it, the more confident I am that I want to spend the rest of my life with this woman. I'll do whatever it takes.

"Be her *friend,* take things slow like you promised. You know, don't stay over at her house after talking for a few days. That's what she asked for, right?" He's acting as if I should know the answer, but it feels wrong. "She doesn't need a man, she's fine on her own. Hell, so is my wife, but she doesn't hold a grudge like Emma does. You're not a man of your word."

"You're not helping right now."

"I warned you this was a mistake, but you didn't listen."
When he pauses, I imagine he's shaking his head in disbelief. "Just play it cool, and don't shower her with hearts and
flowers for the rest of the day. Can you do that?"

I protest, "I don't shower girls with hearts and flowers."

"What do you think you're doing right now? And Emma is
not a girl, she's a woman. Unfortunately, you screwed up so
badly, she might not give you another chance unless you
give her some space to breathe. She doesn't need you in
her life, so you're going to have to work for it. Prove you're
not the same dick you were in your twenties. Show her that
you respect her space."

"I know, I know. It's just that she makes me feel things I
haven't felt in forever. When we were together, she brought
out the best in me… and I screwed it up."

"So, be the person that makes *her* feel things. This isn't
about you." He is definitely Team Emma, which may work
to my advantage.

I think through my options before one comes to me.
"Emma mentioned she rarely has time for herself, so I'll
plan a weekend getaway for us. We used to get away all the
time. I'll get two rooms—so she doesn't feel like it's a sex
thing—but we can spend quality time getting to know each
other again, without our kids."

I'm a genius.

I start looking on my computer for destination ideas, when
he confirms my plan is incredibly brilliant.

Okay, fine, so he agrees it isn't bad. "That's not the worst idea,
especially if you actually have two rooms and give her
some space. But maybe don't tell her about it right away,

feel her out first? You know what I mean? Is she even available? I know she's busy with the boys and working all the time. Don't plan it until you talk to her about it."

"She said her ex has the boys every other weekend from Saturday morning until Monday, except when her son has soccer. Mountain weekend vacation, it's happening."

"*Ugh*, whatever, man. Just leave me out of it. If you tell me details, and Lily asks me, I'll have to tell her. And you know she can't keep a secret."

"Got it, thanks! Are we still on for drinks Thursday after work?"

"You know it."

He hangs up and I sit there for a moment processing everything. Once I've collected myself, I start looking up resorts a few hours from us, determined to make things right. When I find the perfect fit, I open our texts and reply to her message from earlier.

> Absolutely. Can't wait to see you again.

12

EMMA

The week is relatively uneventful: meetings on top of meetings for work, a very productive IEP meeting for Aiden, wine and Pride and Prejudice with Riley and Lily on Tuesday, and a PTA meeting on Thursday night. That's what my life is these days—meetings.

Saturday morning arrives and I'm elated to have a moment to breathe. Noah comes into my bedroom where I'm currently folding a mountain of laundry. "Hey Mom, I'm so sorry! I forgot my book report is due next week, and Charlie is still reading the book, so I can't use it. Can we run to the bookstore and grab another one?"

Noah knows books are my weakness; I'll never say no. "Sure, help me get everyone ready. They open in an hour."

Per usual, I make sure the kids get dressed. I don't bother with myself, and leave the house in my 'mom uniform,' which consists of a messy bun, no makeup, leggings, and the hoodie Dylan bought me. I just hope I don't see anyone I know today.

We load up my minivan and drive to my favorite local bookstore. I'm craving a Thai coconut milk tea boba from the cafe two doors down from the shop, so I tell the boys we're stopping there first. Aiden needs a warning of any routine change, but at the mention of the cafe, he's all too eager to go. I remind myself that I know the cashiers and they won't care if I walk in looking like a hot mess.

As we enter the cafe, Aiden is holding my hand to my right. I never know if today is the day he will feel like it's his time to shine and choose to do something unexpected, like run off. While some triggers are predictable, all it takes is a bad sensory day. Noah wants chocolate milk and Charlie decides on an ice water and a lemon loaf. I always get chocolate chip cookies for Aiden and me.

There is one person in front of us ordering. *Why on earth are they taking four centuries to order a latte?*

Someone grabs my left hand, and I assume, for half a second, that it's Charlie. It's not. It's a much larger hand that squeezes three times. *Dylan.* I gasp and look to my left to confirm, swiftly pulling my hand away; I don't want my boys to know I'm dating again. *Am I dating again?*

I stupidly glance up to find those damn dimples that make my knees buckle. "Oh, hi."

He's with his daughters, who are probably three or four years older than my boys. He doesn't seem to care that I'm with my kids, or that he's with his, and leans in to kiss my cheek.

"Nice sweatshirt, E," he says quietly. He raises his voice a little and explains, "Harriet and Lizzy wanted to pick out a few books and insisted we grab a boba first." Boba is definitely an acquired taste, so I'm curious to see what he orders.

"I wish my kids would drink it, but they say it's too slimy. What's your favorite?"

The older daughter chimes in, "Oh, no. Dad *hates* boba, he only comes for the lemon loaf."

I smile and reply with a chuckle, "I get it. Charlie is obsessed with their lemon loaf here. I like their Thai coconut milk tea, with the larger pearls." She smiles back at me and I continue, "Hi, I'm sorry, it appears I have awful manners. I'm Emma. And these are my boys." I gesture to each of them as I say their names. "Charlie, Noah, and Aiden."

She returns the smile. "I'm Harriet, and my sister Lizzy is over there at the table with her ereader. Wait, did you say Emma? Are you named after the book? Lizzy and I are named after Jane Austen characters."

Dylan wraps his arm around Harriet, interjecting, "Sorry, I didn't think to introduce you. Emma and I are old friends; we've known each other for longer than you've been alive. It's actually because of Emma that you're named Harriet, and Lizzy is Lizzy. She made me watch all the movies with her when we were younger."

I'm rooted in place, in absolute shock. How could he drop that bomb on me, as if it's nothing? Why didn't he mention it the other night when he was talking about his girls?

Harriet rolls her eyes, shrugging his arm off her shoulders. "Whatever, Dad." She looks to me. "So, what's the deal?

My dad doesn't have any friends. Are you guys dating, or something?"

I'm surprised by the question, unsure of how much he told his girls and how to answer it. Dylan chuckles, because of course he finds this funny. Thankfully, my kids aren't paying attention and, before I can answer, the cashier asks for my order.

As we wait for our food and drinks, the kids are at a table talking about fantasy books and video games. I'm surprised to see Aiden talking with them; he doesn't normally like meeting new people. I've been quiet too long and feel I need to fill the silence. "So… big weekend plans?"

What the hell am I doing? I hate small talk.

He leans in. "Well, I wanted to take out this amazing woman I know, but she doesn't have time for me." At first, I think he's upset, but his smile is ear to ear.

"Come on, Dylan, that's not fair. I have the boys this weekend."

His wide grin doesn't falter. "I know, beautiful. I'm teasing. What are you guys up to today?"

I wonder if he's looking for an invite, since his daughter revealed they're also headed there next. As if watching a train wreck in slow motion, I reply, "Just headed to the bookstore. Noah has a book report due. I also wanted to pick up a book duet my friend recommended."

He raises his eyebrow smugly. "What book did your friend recommend?"

I don't want to tell him it's a spicy billionaire romance. Which, quite frankly, is the *last thing* I should be reading right now. I'm able to avoid the question when my name is called out with my order.

Saved by the barista!

As we join our kids at the table next to theirs, Dylan gives me a strange look that I can't place. I can't help asking, "What?"

"I shouldn't tell you, E. We said we were taking things slow and what I was thinking was *definitely not*." Thankfully, his voice is low enough that only I can hear him. He looks over at our kids laughing and… He's right, that's definitely not taking things slow. His gaze comes back to me and he leans in. "I'm playing for keeps, Emma. That right there"—he gestures to our kids—"that's important to me."

I reply with a nod; it's also important to me, which is why we need to take our time with whatever this is. But I can't help but wonder what everything might look like a year or two from now.

"Hey, Mom, can we go now?" Charlie's voice brings me back to the present.

"Sure, let's head out." I begin to stand, but Dylan beats me to pull out my chair. "Thank you."

As the kids are cleaning up, he takes my hand. Knowing they're preoccupied, he squeezes three times before releasing it. "Come on, beautiful, let's go."

We walk together to the bookstore; the twins talking with his girls a few paces in front of us, while Aiden holds my hand. I can tell Dylan is itching to hold my free one, but am grateful he's giving me space in front of my boys.

I lean over, and ask quietly, so only he can hear, "Why didn't you tell me? You named your daughters after Austen characters?"

He shrugs. "I don't know, I figured it would come up eventually."

Thanks for the non-answer, Dylan.

Entering the bookstore, Aiden wants to join his brothers. He's also taken a liking to Lizzy, who seems to be a little introverted, like him. Charlie's already picked out a book and is sitting in one of the comfortable leather chairs—he won't be moving for a while—and Lizzy is looking at the new illustrated fantasy books with Aiden.

Harriet offers, "I want to grab a book over in the YA section, but I can help Noah find his book if you want?"

"If you don't mind, that'd be great," Dylan replies for us, though I can sense he's up to something.

Harriet smiles and replies to Noah directly, "If you like the wizard series we talked about, I have *just* the book for you! Come on."

He looks to me for confirmation and I nod. "Go ahead, I'll be right over there." I gesture to the fiction and romance sections. "If you need anything, come and find me."

As they walk away, I lower my voice so only Dylan can hear. "Okay, I need to move quickly, it's only a matter of time before one of them gets us kicked out of here, or Aiden makes a break for it." I dart to the romance section.

Dylan follows me, glancing over his shoulder at the kids, who are now nearly out of view. He grabs my hand, pulls me down one of the aisles, and backs me up against one of the bookcases. His hands move to either side of me, just above my head.

How do I keep ending up caged in by this guy?

I'm entirely too attracted to the fact that he can go from caring dad to dominating me in such a public place. He closes the distance but stops short of kissing me. Our noses brush, but my hands fly to his chest to keep him from coming closer.

"Dylan, we can't do this, our kids are just a few aisles away."

He pulls back a few inches. His right hand leaves the bookcase behind me as he runs his fingers through his hair, then rests it on my hip. "I know." His expression is now almost pained. "I'm sorry. I'm messing this up."

"No, you're not. It's just really easy to slip into old habits."

"You're right," he sighs. "I'm trying to pick up where we left off, and that's not fair to you."

Moving a hand up his chest, I cup his cheek. "Last weekend was amazing. But I don't want to pick up where we left off. I want to get to know you again, maybe start over." I pause, moving my hand back to his chest, sure he will kiss me if I don't provide a barrier. I continue, "Could we maybe work on being friends? Then see where it goes?"

He chuckles, but his eyes darken. "Emma, I could never just be your friend." Before I can protest, he continues, "But you're right, we should take some time to do this right. What are you doing next weekend?"

"Nothing planned. Kids are at their dad's, and I have a few manuscripts to get through, but that's it."

He's up to something, and he confirms my suspicion. "Come away with me." It isn't a question.

I can't help but laugh. "Come away with you? What happened to taking things slow? What next, you want me to move in with you?" I say it in jest, but with how his eyes are burning into me, he's not taking it as a joke at all.

"Two rooms," he clarifies. "I want to get away for a weekend like we used to. It'll give us a chance to catch up, without distractions."

I ponder his proposal for a second, knowing it's a terrible idea, but I want to give him the benefit of the doubt. "Deal. If, and only if, I have my own room." I find myself getting lost in his eyes when he looks at me like this.

Without realizing it, my hands travel down his chest to his waist. I don't think much of it, until he murmurs, "*Fuck.*"

Dylan moves his hand from the shelf, a caress of his fingers pass my shoulder to my neck before wrapping his hand around the front of it. I can't help the moan that escapes me as he squeezes gently, pulling me in for a bruising kiss. It's demanding and *definitely* not appropriate for a book-store. It also isn't the sweet way he used to kiss me when we were younger. I melt into his touch as he teases and tastes, exploring my mouth as if he's trying to memorize every part of me. I kiss him back harder, not caring that someone might catch me kissing him with my back pressed up against the bookshelves.

When he breaks away, I'm completely out of breath. He rests his forehead on mine and moves his hand from my neck to my heart; I brush my fingers over my now-plump lips.

"Sorry, I've been wanting to do that since I left your house Monday." He clears his throat. "Well, let's grab this book your friend told you to read, and then we should probably find our kids."

Right, we both came here with kids, but the way he said it was like they were *ours* together. My back is still against the bookcase and this hardly looks innocent. He notices too and takes my hand, squeezing it three times as he leads me down the aisle. I glance up to question if he meant to do that, and find his beautiful blue eyes already on me. A small smirk tugs at his lips. He told me he'll take things slow, but if today is any indication, that is definitely *not* happening.

I grab the book duet *Whiskey Lies* and *Loving Whiskey* by Brittanée Nicole from the shelves. He eyes it curiously and asks, "This is it?"

Smiling, I shrug. "Yeah, it's supposed to be good. A few of my friends recommended it." There's no way in hell I'm telling him that one of them also said it's the hottest billionaire book she's read in the last year. He snatches one out of my hand. "Hey!"

He raises an eyebrow and opens the book to a random page and begins reading aloud. "*There isn't a moment in time when I don't want you, when I won't drop everything I'm doing to pleasure you.*" My cheeks heat and are likely a bright crimson as my eyes dart to either side of us to ensure no one is eavesdropping. He closes the book and lowers his voice, "Emma, Emma, Emma. Should we read these together next weekend?"

I gasp and steal the book back. "No, absolutely not!"

He chuckles. "I'll just have to get my own copy then."

I stop him as he tries to pick up a second set. "Why don't I just lend you mine when I'm done? I doubt you want your daughters to see you buying these. They are trophy books anyway. I'll be reading on my ereader."

Realizing I have a point, he puts them back. "Just so you know, I could have written those words myself." Then, he winks at me.

Ugh, what am I going to do with him? So much for keeping my wits about me.

We find our kids, who are scattered throughout the store. Thankfully, Aiden is safe with Noah and Harriet. I really shouldn't have let Dylan distract me like that. He tries to buy all of our books, but I'm faster with my card to buy mine. My kids can sense something is up, so I rush us out of the store and to our cars.

On the way home, I spot a new text from him. Once I'm parked, I open my messages, clicking on the text from Dylan.

DYLAN

I'll pick you up at six on Friday. Pack for 60° weather.

What are you up to, Dylan?

13

DYLAN

I haven't stopped thinking about that kiss with Emma on Saturday—the little breath she sucked in when I bit her bottom lip, the way she let me take what I wanted as she melted into me, the blush on her neck and cheeks when I read from her book, how she whimpered in protest when I broke our kiss...

Fuck.

Emma never kissed me like that when we were together, it was always so safe and wholesome. She was always the girl-next-door type; I was always afraid I'd corrupt her. This Emma, though, she's strong and stubborn, but she allowed me to claim a piece of her as mine. It made me wonder just how much I can push her, how much she might surrender to me if given the chance. I saw the way she looked at me at the game, how her breath hitched when I called her a good girl. What I wouldn't give to have her laid out for me, tied up and begging to come.

The kiss two days ago was easily the best of my life, even if it wasn't nearly enough. I can't imagine kissing another woman ever again and it took everything in me to not take things further. At one point, I forgot I was in a damn bookstore.

She wants to take things slow, and I really tried. The minute she agreed to go away with me, my mind was taken over with the thoughts of having her all to myself for a few days. I lost it.

I should have been working this morning, spending the majority of my time researching cabins in the mountains for us to stay at next weekend. There's one right on the lake but it only has one bedroom. I promised her two, so I called the travel company and reserved a cabin that's a little further from the water. Whatever my girl wants, she'll…

What the hell am I saying? She's not mine.

Yet.

When I got home Saturday evening, I ordered violets to be delivered to her office today. I don't care what Andrew says; I want Emma to know I'm thinking of her. I also needed a reason to talk to her. My plan comes to fruition when I receive an incoming text from her.

> EMMA
>
> The flowers are incredibly thoughtful, thank you.

> You're welcome. Are you ready for this weekend?

> Not sure, you haven't told me where we're going…

> I intend on keeping it a surprise until the moment we arrive.

> Fine, but I have a surprise of my own that you won't know until we arrive.

> I'll tell, if you tell?

> Okay, on 3. 1... 2... 3

> Cabin in the mountains.

> Well... what's yours?

> My fingers were crossed behind my back. I'm not telling. You'll have to find out for yourself.

This woman's always keeping me on my toes.

> Can I have a hint?

> Nope. See you Friday!

> Wait, you're not going to talk to me until Friday?

> Well, that's what "see you Friday" implies.

Instead of texting back, I call. After two rings, she picks up.

"To what do I owe the pleasure of this call, Mr. Alexander?"

Fuck, I love it when she calls me that.

"Well, I was wondering why you're making me wait five days to talk to you again?" At this point, there's no way I could go a single day without hearing her voice.

"What's five days when we haven't talked for over a decade?"

She has a point. I counter, "The difference is you never kissed me the way you did at the bookstore, or the game, when we were younger."

"I, uh, don't know what you mean." Her voice is a little shaky, and I love that I can rile her up so easily.

"You know exactly what I mean. You say you want to take things slow, but when you kiss me back like that," I almost groan. "Now all I want to do is drive over to your office and taste every inch of your body to see if it's still as sweet as I remember."

Like a shot of honey—pure and addicting.

She coughs, choking on her drink, which makes me think of other things she might choke on. I have to adjust myself, and once she collects herself, she hisses, "Dylan! I'm at work! You can't say stuff like that to me!"

"What? I can't talk about how I could drop by around lunch, place you on your desk, hike up your skirt and feast on you until you come on my tongue?"

"How can you expect me to go back to work right now? Come on! *Ugh*, I should never have picked up the phone, I have a meeting in ten minutes."

Say the word and I'll make sure we christen every surface of your office, E.

I can't help seeing exactly how far she'll let me tease her. "Are you wet, Emma?"

"I don't think that's any of your business. But after that little—whatever that was—I'm keeping to my word and not talking to you until Friday." She's flustered, but I know that if dropped by as I suggested, I would have her coming in minutes.

"Or, I can come by tonight?"

"I'm hanging up now!" There's playfulness in her tone that I haven't heard in a while.

I make sure to lower my voice as I tell her, "See you Friday, beautiful."

I hear her shifting in her seat. "Yup, Friday." She hangs up on me.

Dylan - 1, Emma - 0.

Who am I kidding? This woman has me wrapped around her finger.

14

EMMA

I'm wound so tight, I feel like I'm about to explode. How am I supposed to spend a weekend with this man who can't keep his hands off me whenever we're together?

Do I even want him to keep his hands off me?

I shouldn't be complaining. This is every girl's dream—a hot possessive man who wants to do naughty things to you. Only one problem: It's Dylan. I fell for him so hard all those years ago and I can't forget how broken I was when it ended. I'm deathly afraid it will happen again.

As I set my phone down, it lights up with a text. Thinking it's Dylan again, I open my messages.

> **ETHAN**
>
> Hey babe! Sorry I've been MIA. We picked up a few last minute events and it's been insanely busy.
>
> How was your date at the baseball game? Miss you!

Damn, I miss him. Ethan's been my best friend since college. Even though he's a self-made millionaire, owning one of the biggest event planners in the area, no matter how busy he gets, he always makes time for me. He's been sending me random memes throughout the week until we can get together for drinks or coffee. They always make me smile and brighten my day.

We dated for a few weeks, nearly two decades ago, before very quickly discovering that we were better off friends. He knows me better than any of my girlfriends, but also remembers how Dylan broke my heart. When I told him about the date, he wasn't as enthusiastic about it as the girls were.

> Hey, handsome! It went well. Probably too well. He invited me on a trip next weekend.

> What? No, Em, you can't. He's a wanker who just wants to get his dick wet.

> Wanker? Trying on British slang this week?

> I promoted Tyler. I've spent a bit of time with him the last few weeks training him to be an event manager. He's from somewhere across the pond and it must be rubbing off on me.

> Did Dylan ever tell you why he ghosted you? I thought you were going to marry him before he pulled that shit.

> Across the pond? Seriously, who says that? Also, no, we haven't talked about it.

> Don't go on a trip with someone who is proof that evolution can be reversed.

I can't help but laugh. Ethan has always had the most colorful insults for Dylan. I should prepare for them to escalate now that I'm dating Dylan, again. *Are we dating, again?* It feels like Dylan and I fast-tracked our way into some sort of situationship.

> You know, I think you're just jealous and want to keep me all to yourself.

> Guilty as charged. You'll always be my girl.

I send him an eye roll emoji and set my phone to *do not disturb*. Maybe Ethan's right, I need to get to the bottom of what happened all those years ago.

Two days later, Ethan's words are still eating away at me. *"Did Dylan ever tell you why he ghosted you after dating for eight months?"* Curiosity gets the better of me and I message Dylan.

> Free for a call tonight?

DYLAN

> Absolutely, I'm free any time for you.

When I get home, I go through the evening bedtime routine for my kids on autopilot. After getting ready for bed myself and changing into my pajamas—an oversized tee and underwear—I struggle to muster up the courage to call him. Part of me doesn't want the truth, but Ethan is right; we should get it out in the open before spending a weekend together.

I pour myself a glass of wine and set the door alarm before walking back up to my room. Settling into my bed with my reading pillow behind me, I scroll social media for a few minutes, procrastinating. I blow out a deep breath, click on my call logs, and hover over his name for a moment before finally pressing it. It rings three times before he picks up.

"Hey, beautiful. How was your day?"

I'm so nervous to have this conversation, I don't even say hello. Instead, I blurt, "What happened sixteen years ago?"

He pauses. "What do you mean?"

"What do you mean, what do I mean? You know what I mean." My voice is carrying, and lower it a little just in case I sound shrill. "You literally disappeared after we dated for almost a year. No 'hey babe, it's not working out' or 'I'm seeing someone else.'" I sigh, though it comes out as a groan. "It was so embarrassing."

"You want the truth?" He says it so matter of factly, it gives me pause.

"No, just lie to me to make me feel better," I quip.

He chuckles to himself, but still taking me seriously, replies, "E, I fucked up. We were kids, and I was scared. You're the kind of woman a man spends forever with—complete with the white picket fence and two-point-five kids."

"So, you punished me for, what? Being a good girlfriend?" I'm quickly regretting not pouring a second glass of wine for this conversation.

"You want me to be honest with you, but I don't want you to hate me for it."

"I deserve the truth, Dylan."

He blows out a long breath. "I know I sound like a total asshole, but... We were young, and I wanted to date around a little more, to be sure you really were the one. Which, in hindsight, was the stupidest fucking idea I ever came up with, because it was always supposed to be you and me. No one could hold a candle to you. But by the time I figured out what an idiot I was, you had blocked my number and moved on."

I pause for a moment, taking in what he just told me. "I wasn't enough," I mumble to myself, feeling my heart break all over again.

"Emma, you can't be serious! You were *always* enough. I was just too young and dumb to see that what I had was absolute perfection. I know it was a shitty move, and you didn't deserve what I did to you. There isn't a day that has gone by that I haven't thought of you, regretted what I did, and wondered how things would be so different if I wasn't such a jackass in my twenties. We're both different people now; let me prove to you that I'm not the same man I was, that I'm a better man who will work every day to deserve you."

"I don't know if I should come this weekend." The words spill from my lips before I can stop them.

"I would never hurt you again." His voice is pleading, it twists my heart. "What would it take for you to change your mind? To give us a chance?"

At hearing his words, my eyes fill with unshed tears. "You hurt me more than any other man I've ever known. How am I supposed to trust that, in a year, you're not just going to get bored with me, and disappear off the face of the planet again? Or worse, not have the decency to leave me before you move on to greener pastures? We aren't kids anymore. I don't know if I could take you breaking me again."

"E, listen to me." His voice is soft but commanding—a lethal combination. "I don't know the future. What I do know is that you were *always* the one. I know you feel it too. You're scared, but we both know it's supposed to be you and me in the end. I'm so sorry I hurt you. I can't erase the past, but I would give anything for you to forgive me, to give us a second chance. I promise I'll never do anything to hurt you, ever again." There's the sound of a car door closing and the familiar beep of someone locking their car outside; it echoes through the phone. "Open your front door, Emma."

"You're here?"

"Please, open the door." His voice cracks.

I hang up and rush downstairs, my phone still in my hand. Once I get to the front door, even knowing it's Dylan, I check the peephole. My heart stops as soon as I see him pacing, running his hands through his hair. I glance down at my inappropriate attire for this conversation. *Well, he's seen me naked before. Pants can wait.* With a deep breath, I open it for him after disabling the alarm. "Dylan, what are you doing here?"

Dylan glances down, noticing my lack of pants and shakes his head. "I was down the street, about to run into the grocery store. I stayed in my car to take the call, until you started asking about the past. I don't know, I just felt like we should talk about this in person... maybe with pants on?" He quirks an eyebrow.

"Well, how was I supposed to know you were going to drop by?" I take his hand in mine and tug him into the house. "The kids are asleep, we need to keep our voices down."

Closing the door behind us, he sets my alarm for me, never letting go of my hand. Tucking my hair behind my ear, he asks, "Can I show you something?"

I nod, but he begins leading me to the stairs, and I stop him. "Dylan, you're not staying the night. My kids are home. In fact, we aren't going anywhere near my bedroom. I should put pants on, though."

Dylan chuckles and stops me from heading upstairs. "I know, I won't stay long, but I'm not letting you sneak away upstairs, either. If I'm not allowed up there, then I'll improvise." With a smirk, he pulls me into the kitchen and turns on the light. Once we reach the island, he surprises me by lifting me by the waist and setting me on the counter. He stands between my legs, giving me flashbacks of the last time he was here.

Totally should have put on pants.

Pulling me to the edge, I'm nearly straddling him. My heart is pounding and, being this close to him, I ache everywhere. His familiar musk of leather and embers envelops me. *Or it's just the candle I bought recently because it reminded me of him.*

He settles my hand over his heart, holding it in place. "This is yours, E. It always has been, and always will be." Tears threaten to betray me with little pricks behind my eyes. "I'm not perfect, but I need you to know that you are it for me. That's why I wanted to go away this weekend. It's not to pick up where we left off. You were right, we need to start over."

I lean my forehead to his, close my eyes, and blow out a long, deep breath. "I'm scared."

"I'm not. Not anymore. I'm only scared of losing you again."

I want to trust him and I'm tired of fighting whatever this is between us. Ready to take the leap, I make the first move. Cupping my hands behind his neck, I pull him in to kiss me. At first, it's slow and soft, full of promises. Sliding his hand into my hair, he wraps it around his fist and tugs back, trailing kisses along my chin until he reaches my ear, nipping the lobe. I miss him touching me like this, being consumed by him. Every reason I had to run has left the room without me. His mouth travels down to my neck, and as he continues peppering kisses, it sends a wave of arousal all over my body.

"I missed you," I admit mostly to myself, but loud enough for him to hear.

As he kisses the small space between my neck and shoulder, he pauses. "Emma, you need to tell me to stop... *right now.*"

Confused, I pull away. "Why?"

"Because I more than just missed you. I need you more than I need to breathe. I don't want to be a gentleman, and I sure as hell don't want to take things slow right now. I swear, I can't think straight when I'm with you. When it's just you and me, nothing else exists. I know we should put the brakes on... but *fuck*, I also want to be deep inside you and hear you scream my name as you come for me."

Dylan softly, slowly caresses my thighs before gripping them. He's losing control and it makes my breath hitch in anticipation. I'm not sure I can handle an unleashed Dylan.

My heart skips a beat, and with a rumble reverberating in his chest, he continues, "I want to wake up every single morning with your beautiful, naked body draped over me before I bury my face between your legs, so I can taste you on my lips the rest of the day. I'm a selfish man. I don't just want you, I want *all of you*. I want to claim every part of you as mine." He cups my cheek, eyes full of so much hope. "Do you have any idea what you do to me? It's only been this way with you. No one ever came close."

His hard length presses against my center, wringing a moan from both of us. I want him, more than I should if I want to protect myself from getting hurt. I'm fed up with the war between my head and my heart. My forehead collapses against his chest as I fist his shirt to pull him closer.

I let out a groan before I finally find my voice, even if it's a whisper, "Dylan, my kids are upstairs."

His grip on my thighs loosens as he sighs. "I know, E. I know."

"No, I don't think you do." I pull him back to me, wanting him close. "Do you have any idea what you do to *me?* I've wanted you for years. I don't want you to stop. But... my kids are upstairs and you know I can't be quiet when it comes to you."

Dylan huffs a small laugh, a smirk tugging at his lips. "Oh, I remember."

Biting my lip, I fight memories from sixteen years ago, knowing exactly what this man is capable of. *I'm on my counter… in my underwear… and all I want to do is touch him.* I reach between us, stroking his cock slowly through his pants. I want him tonight, even if I can't have all of him right now.

He tightens his grip on my thighs again and growls, "Emma, what are you doing?"

"What does it look like I'm doing? I want to feel you." I should hate how desperate I sound, but I can't help how my whole body is lit up at his touch.

His hand envelops my wrist to stop me. "Baby, I am not coming in your hand." He brings the inside of my wrist to his lips. "The next time I come with you, I'll be balls deep inside you, only after I've worshiped and tasted every inch of your incredible body. But more importantly, when I'm promised seconds and thirds, and even that won't be enough."

I'm so incredibly turned on, but where does this leave us if he won't let me touch him?

Dylan kisses my forehead and demands, "Lie down, beautiful."

"On my counter? Are you insane?" I whisper-shout. "We are *not* having sex in my kitchen."

His eyes dark with lust, he insists, "Be my good girl and lie down." The commanding words wash over me, making me shudder. I lean back on my elbows as he slips off my panties, stuffing them in his pocket. "You listen so well, baby. Do you have any idea how gorgeous you are? Can I touch you?" I nod, biting my lip. He runs two of his fingers up and down my slit before hooking them inside me. His touch sends sparks across my entire body. "So wet and ready for me. I miss having you like this whenever I want," he murmurs before slowly removing his fingers and sucking them clean. "Fuck, I forgot how incredible you taste."

My head falls back as Dylan kisses the inside of my thighs, and I can't help the moan that escapes me. His hands on me feel so familiar, but new at the same time.

"Eyes on me, baby." It startles me, but I comply. "Attagirl, I want to see those beautiful blue eyes when you fall apart." He continues kissing closer and closer to where I need him. The scruff of his five o'clock shadow scratches the inside of my thigh, making me ache for him to put his mouth on my clit. "What do you want, Emma? Name it, and it's yours." As I'm about to reply, he licks up my pussy, causing my body to tremble.

"I… I want you." They're the only words I can get out.

"You have me, beautiful." He continues teasing, licking small, firm circles around my clit.

"*Dylan*," I whimper as my orgasm quickly builds. I haven't been touched by a man in over a year. It only takes a minute, two tops, before his talented tongue has me seeing stars behind my eyes and wave after wave of pleasure rips through my body. Watching him with his face between my legs is such an erotic experience, I can't help the moaning. I do my best to stifle them, but fail. He slows his pace as I come down from the euphoria.

"Do you know long I have dreamt of having you laid out for me like this? So fucking beautiful. Let me take one more from you."

"My legs are jelly. I can hardly move." I don't remember

the last time I had two back-to-back, except with my vibrator.

He smiles, teasing my entrance before he hooks his fingers inside in one swift movement. "You're mine, Emma. If I say I'm taking one more, then you're coming for me one more time."

I sit up, grab the collar of his shirt and pull him in to kiss me. Between kisses, the words tumble from my lips without thought to their meaning, "*Yours.*"

If I thought I'd seen Dylan lose control, I was wrong. "Mine," he growls as he pushes his fingers deeper inside me. I let out a stifled moan; trying to keep quiet is proving to be very difficult. I tighten around him as he groans against my lips, "That's it, baby, I know you're close again. Let go for me." His thumb presses harder as he circles my clit, his fingers curling at the perfect pace and pressure. "You're absolutely stunning when you give yourself to me." His words push me over the edge as the crash of my second orgasm hits. My body is buzzing, my limbs weak, and I can't stop kissing him as he helps me come down. My whimper slips out as he moves his mouth down my body, slowly and tenderly, before landing just above my clit. "Let's see how many times I can make you come before I need to leave."

I don't want his mouth again, I want *him*.

"Wait, Dylan. I know I said no sex. I lied. I need you. I need you *right now*."

"No, not tonight, baby." He chuckles and his smile couldn't be wider. "Tonight was just me confirming something."

My brows pinch. "What's that?"

"After all this time, you're still mine. You, reacting to my touch like this, so responsive… It's the most beautiful thing I've ever seen."

"Why won't you let me touch you?"

"Because this isn't just sex. I've never had this kind of connection with anyone else. Only you. I know you want me as much as I want you; I don't need to come, to prove that. You're mine, just as I've always been yours."

Shit. I did say I was his, didn't I? It was kind of in the heat of the moment. Now that the brain fog from my orgasm has lifted and reality is crashing into me, it feels a bit like rejection, and I desperately want to change the subject. I know in my heart he's right, I need my head to catch up, and that's going to take some time.

I clear my throat. "So, what was it you were going to show me earlier?"

Dylan kisses the inside of my thigh and moves his way up my body until his lips brush my neck. He murmurs against my skin, "Sorry, I got distracted by a beautiful woman who opened the door with no pants on. How could I not want to touch you? Come on, where's your closest mirror?"

After he helps me off the counter, I guide him to the downstairs guest room that has a full length mirror in the corner. He stands behind me as we both face it.

"Okay, now what?"

He wraps his arms around me, resting his chin on my shoulder. "This, baby. This is what I wanted to show you."

I'm so confused, but *damn*, it feels too good to be in his

arms. "I'm sorry to ruin whatever you're trying to do here, but I have no idea what you're getting at."

"I told you: You were meant for me." He kisses my shoulder and tightens his arms around me. "I want you to see for yourself how you still fit so perfectly in my arms, as if no time has passed. You're mine. We can stop pretending we don't belong to each other."

I lean my head back. "You can't keep saying stuff like that."

"Why not? It's the truth. Afraid you might fall in love with me again? We said we would take things slow, but I'm yours, E. I'm not going anywhere. If I push too hard, I need you to tell me, and not retreat to that mind palace of yours. I lost you once, and I'll be damned if I lose you again." He continues kissing my neck, our eyes meeting in our reflection.

"You won't run away if I take too long to get to where you're at?"

"Me, run? I'm afraid you're the one that's going to run this time." I glance down, laughing at the truth in his statement. "Eyes on me, baby." My gaze snaps up immediately to meet his in the mirror. "Come away with me this weekend, so I can show you this isn't just physical for me. I promise you'll have your own space there." He nips at my earlobe. "But If you're okay with it, tonight, I don't want to take my hands off you. I want one more before I go."

His hand drifts down my stomach, lifting up my oversized shirt slightly, and slides two fingers between my legs. My eyes never leave Dylan as he takes what's his.

15

DYLAN

The rest of the week, I'm lost in flashbacks of Emma writhing beneath me, coming hard on my hand and tongue, looking even more exquisite than I remember. I swear I can still taste her. I didn't want to push her too far; if we slept together, she could have freaked out and bailed on the weekend. As much as she says she wanted to, I know better.

I love that, after all this time, I still have her body memorized. I want to claim her, brand her, own her... all of her. Permanently. She isn't there yet, but ever since that moment in the bookstore when she joked about moving in, I can't stop thinking about it. I would marry her tomorrow if she was ready. After everything I put her through when we were younger, I don't blame her for being cautious. If the situation was reversed, I would want to take things slow, too.

Before I left her house, I carried her up to bed and tucked her in before cleaning up the mess we made in her kitchen and guest room. She could barely move after her third orgasm and I wanted to take care of her. *She's mine to take care of now.* The thought grounds me. I would've stayed the night if I didn't have to get home to the girls. They're old enough to be left alone for a little while, but not overnight.

It's Friday, and I'm counting down the hours until I get to see her again. Not just because I've fantasized the last few nights about how tight she is and how she'll feel wrapped around my cock—though that's certainly part of it. I fully intend to spend the weekend winning her back.

After work, I stop by my house to grab my duffel bag for the weekend. I pull out a box of condoms from my bedside table, only to pause before tucking them in my bag. *Do I bring them?* I don't think we'll use them, but I don't want to be unprepared either. I promised her two rooms, no matter how much I want her in my bed, tangled up in each other the whole weekend. I take out a few and place them in the zippered compartment of my duffle. *Just in case.*

I pick up coffee on the way over to her house. Knocking lightly a few times, she opens the door, and I'm speechless. She's fucking breathtaking; wearing a skin-tight black dress that hugs every delicious curve of her body.

Emma greets me with a soft smile. "Hey, so sorry, I'm running behind. I haven't had a chance to change. Do you mind coming in for a minute?" She opens the door wider for me to enter.

As I walk in, I lean in to kiss her cheek. She hums, almost a whimper, disappointed that it was only her cheek. *Me too, E. Me too.* I itch to back her up against the door, spread her legs, and take what's mine again. Once the door is closed, she asks me to stay downstairs while she gets dressed. I set our coffees on the counter and pull out my phone to check the traffic for the drive.

A few minutes later, she comes back down in the hoodie I bought her and a pair of black leggings, similar to the ones she wore to the bookstore that leave nothing to the imagination. I chuckle to myself. "E, you can't wear those."

I fucking adore this woman—she knows *exactly* what she's doing. I'm moments away from pulling her legs around me and hauling her upstairs. It's too fucking tempting. We aren't in the bookstore or any other public place. Fuck the cabin. I want to rip those sorry excuse for pants off her right now, bury my face between her legs again, make her scream my name as she—

"What do you mean? I want to be comfortable." She glances down at her pants, but I still spot the little smirk she's hiding. I grab her hand and march her gorgeous ass back upstairs. "Dylan, what are you doing? We need to go."

"You can pretend that you don't know how incredibly sexy you are in those pants, but we both know what you're doing. I can't be in the car for a few hours with you wearing those, and keep my hands off you. Either they come off right now and you sit on my face, or you change."

"Oh, come on! They're just leggings!"

We pause at her bedroom door. "Your choice, E."

She rolls her eyes. "Fine, give me two minutes, and I'll meet you downstairs… again. Now, shoo or we'll never leave." I contemplate stripping her out of them myself for a moment, but agree and return downstairs.

When she comes down the second time, she's a pair of tight jeans like the ones she wore when we went to the game. They make her ass look amazing. That night, it felt so right staying over, holding her in my arms for the first time in years. She always was the perfect fit. The sight of her wearing them makes my cock twitch. *Down boy.*

I clear my throat and hand her the coffee I brought her. "Ready?"

Emma pauses before she takes a sip, curiously looking up at me through her lashes. "What did you get me?"

I shrug. "That pumpkin drink you always used to order this time of year, but with oat milk." I noticed her creamer was non-dairy; I'm not sure if it's a preference or allergy, but figured it was a safe bet.

Her smile wide, she lifts onto the balls of her feet to kiss me on the cheek. "Thank you, I really need it after the long week I've had."

"Want to talk about it?"

"No." She shakes her head. "Not right now. We should get going."

We load up the car and once we are on the road, I ask again, "So, what happened this week? Anything fun?"

She tries to hide it, but her eyes widen and her cheeks flush. "You mean, since I last saw you? It's been… busy." I can only hope she was thinking of the other night. I sure as hell haven't stopped thinking about it. I plan on reminding her she's mine as often as possible, just to see that beautiful blush of hers.

As we pull up to the next stop light, I turn toward her. Interlacing our fingers, I brush a kiss to the back of her hand. My eyes never leave hers, as I quietly tell her, "I don't think I got anything done. I couldn't stop thinking about how gorgeous you look when you come." The light turns green and I lean back against the seat, keeping her hand in mine. She sucks in a breath, and I briefly glance over; her cheeks are my favorite shade of crimson.

Emma finally breaks her silence and asks, "So, where exactly are we going?"

I tsk. "Like I would tell you! You still owe me a secret, since you claim your fingers were crossed behind your back."

"Aw, come on! I promise I'll show you tonight!"

I quirk an eyebrow. "Show me?"

"Yup," she says, popping the 'p.'

I let out a light chuckle. "Fine." I check the GPS and notice we're about to hit traffic. I offer, "Are you hungry? We can stop."

She smiles brightly. "Starving." The unmistakable glimmer in her eyes says she isn't just hungry for dinner. This is going to be a long drive if she keeps looking at me that way.

We pull off the freeway, grab dinner at a small diner, and head back on the road. Emma puts on an audiobook of a murder mystery she's been wanting to listen to and I'm grateful for the distraction—and that it wasn't one of her romance books. As we drive, I find myself fantasizing about what our life will look like a few years from now, taking trips like this with our kids or just the two of us.

If I'm not careful, I'll scare her away. Andrew's right, I need to slow down, even if it's the last thing I want to do.

A couple hours later, we arrive at the reception building at the resort. I grab her rolling suitcase and sling my duffle over my shoulder.

She tries to take the suitcase from me, but I insist, "Absolutely not, E," shaking my head. Once inside, we make our way to the check-in area. When it's our turn, I give the receptionist my name on the reservation.

"Ah yes, I have it here. Two bedroom cabin." She types for longer than I would expect, frowning. "Unfortunately, it seems that we overbooked this weekend, but I can offer you an upgrade to one of our lakeside cabins that are right on the water."

"Oh, sure, that would be great. Thank you," I tell her, but then remember my promise to make sure there were two rooms—I don't remember the lakeside cabins having two. Clearing my throat, I ask, "Sorry, I just want to confirm, we'll still have two bedrooms?"

She shakes her head. "No, but the couch in the living room has a sofa bed."

"Okay, that'll work." I pull out my card.

Emma confirms, "That's totally fine. I'll take the couch."

The fuck you are.

"Nice try, beautiful, you'll take the couch when hell freezes over."

The receptionist is visibly uncomfortable, but Emma giggles, shaking her head. "Oh my gosh, I should have seen this coming! Classic."

I frown at her. "What?"

"Oh, come on, you know, the one-bed trope." The receptionist laughs with Emma, but I have no fucking idea what she's talking about. "Dylan, I know you didn't plan it, but I've read this in no less than fifty books." She's still laughing when the receptionist hands my card back. I sign for incidentals and get keys, still a little lost about this inside joke she has with a stranger. But, if it's in a romance book that ends in a happily ever after, I'll gladly take part in whatever this trope entails.

We walk along a paved trail for about five minutes before we reach the cabin. Once inside, I set our bags near the front door and take her hand to lead her to the back porch. It has an amazing view of the lake. Emma tucks into my side, wrapping her arms tightly around my middle while we look out on the water. I can't help holding her tighter and breathing her in as I kiss the top of her head.

"This is incredible, I could live here," she sighs, snuggling closer.

I could live here with you, Emma.

"Yeah. Incredible," I echo, looking at her, not the lake.

I don't want to let her go, but it's getting cold, so I settle for keeping my hand on the small of her back to guide her inside to get warm. We close the door, and I grab my duffel bag to pull out a bottle of wine and a small bag.

Emma's lips tilt up in a small smirk. "What's in there?"

I take out two ereaders; she already has one, but these two are both linked to my account. "One for you and one for me. I loaded a few books on there."

Her eyes light up in appreciation and disbelief. "Why? I don't understand. You know I have one; I brought it with me."

"I know, but you're an especially difficult woman to buy for." Shrugging, I unwrap one of them and power it on before handing it to her. "This way, we can read the same books, and I'll be able to see what you highlight." I playfully wiggle my brows at her, which makes her chuckle.

Emma looks through the library on it, and has likely found the series she bought a physical copy of at the bookstore last weekend, as well as a few new releases from authors I know she loves. My internet stalking proved to be quite useful. Her eyes brighten even more and her smile widens. "This is too much." She gestures to the cabin around us.

I move closer and wrap my arms around her waist, bringing her body flush with mine. Goosebumps travel up my arms as she wraps hers around my neck. I reach behind me to take the ereader out of her hand, and set it on the table. It's been too long since I've kissed her. I glide my fingers into her hair as I bring her lips to mine. It's the sweet and loving kiss I remember from when we were younger—safe and comfortable. Our tongues explore each other's mouths as if no time has passed. I guide her exactly where I want to deepen the kiss; I want more of the Emma from the other night. I slide my hand up her side, still over her hoodie, grazing the underside of her breast, except…

"Emma," I growl, "are you not wearing a bra?"

I'm pretty sure he just growled at me. And no, I'm not wearing a bra. Honestly, it was purely for comfort; I didn't want to be in the car with an underwire poking me for hours. It's bad enough I had to wear jeans.

I offer a sweet smile but his gaze burns into me. "No, why would I?"

Dylan runs his hands down my side and slips them under my sweatshirt, slowly sliding his fingers up until he grazes my peaked nipples. My entire body ignites under his touch.

"*Fuck.*" His dark voice elicits a whimper from me. "The whole ride here, I could have been touching you like this?"

I laugh and attempt to make light of it. "Logistically, it might not have worked, with you driving and all. But yes, *hypothetically*, you could have had your hands under my shirt and would have discovered I'm not wearing a bra." I shrug, but I knew the risk when I chose not to wear one. "I wanted to be comfortable."

"Smart ass." Dylan pinches one of my nipples, and I suck in a breath. Quicker than I can process, he removes his hands from under my shirt, lowers his body, and hoists me up and over his shoulder.

"Hey, put me down," I playfully swat his back as he takes me into the other room.

Dylan tosses me onto the bed and towers over me, placing one hand on either side of my head. I'm pretty sure caging me in is a favorite pastime of his now.

"Take it off." It isn't a question, he demands it.

The control and command in his voice send a shiver down my spine. I do as he asks, pulling my sweatshirt and tee over my head, then shaking my hair out after tossing them to the ground. I can feel him everywhere, even if he isn't touching me yet. His hands move to my thighs. He squeezes once, then hooks his fingers behind my knees and tugs up, forcing my back onto the bed.

"Fuck, Emma, you're so fucking beautiful. Let me see all of you, baby."

And… now I'm wet.

While I'm self-conscious about my body—especially after three kids—when he looks at me like this with so much hunger in his eyes, any and all negative thoughts leave me. I can't find my words, so I just nod. He unbuttons my pants, slowly unzips them, then slides my jeans and panties down my legs. Lowering himself to his knees, he kisses the inside of my thigh.

"Do you have any idea how sexy you are?" He pauses. "Emma… you weren't waxed when I saw you a few days ago."

I can't help the laugh that escapes me. "Surprise!" A rumble comes from his chest before he stands to leave the room. I prop myself onto my elbows, eyes widening. "Hey! Excuse me, Mr. Alexander, but where do you think you're going? You can't just strip me down, tell me I'm pretty, then walk out!" Yes, I called him that with the sole purpose of getting his attention.

He pivots and comes back to me, shaking his head. Pressing a chaste kiss to my lips, he murmurs against them, "I'll be right back; need to grab my bag."

I lay back down and groan. "Seriously?"

After what seems like an eternity, he returns with his bag, sets it down at the foot of the bed, and pulls out the same store bag from earlier.

"Dylan, please don't take this the wrong way, but I'm *not* in the mood to read right now."

He lets out a hearty laugh, removing what looks like an eye mask for sleep. "Do you trust me?"

Do I? I know he would never do anything to hurt me physically. Emotionally? That's another story. Still, I reply, "Yes."

Dylan unwraps the package, pulling out the silk mask. "I want you to feel everything. If we block out one or more of your senses, it'll be more intense." I've read about this, but never tried it. Instinctively, I lean forward in anticipation. He lifts me so my head is on the pillow and softly kisses my lips before he puts the mask over my eyes. "Is this okay, baby?"

I nod.

"No, E, I need your words. I need to know if something is too much, you want more, you want me to stop, or if you need a break."

My voice is quiet. "Yes, it's okay."

"Good girl, now show me how you touch yourself when you're thinking of me."

He never talked like this when we were together. I'm so turned on by this commanding and confident version of him, I'd probably do anything he asked of me. My legs hang open, my fingers find my swollen clit, drawing lazy circles. He peppers kisses down my neck, my chest, then to one of my nipples where he swirls his tongue before taking it in his mouth. His thumb grazes the other and I let out a whimpered moan as he switches.

"What do you think about when you touch yourself?"

I'm consumed by the feeling of his hot breath is a stark contrast to the cool room, I nearly miss the question. "When you used to come by on your lunch break because you couldn't wait until after work to be inside me."

Dylan chuckles against my chest. "You're a gorgeous liar, but I admit I've thought about doing it again recently."

"It's not a lie." He grazes my nipple with his teeth, and I suck in a sharp breath. "It's the darkness in your eyes when you look like you're about to devour me. I come thinking about it. You still get that look, and that's when I know I'm in trouble." There's a good chance he's looking at me that way right now, even if I can't see him.

He reaches between my legs, stopping my movement and replacing my hand with his. I whimper beneath his touch. He groans against my chest, "Oh, you're definitely in trou-

ble. It's my turn, baby. Fuck, look at you. So ready for me."
Moving down my body, he continues pressing soft kisses—
my chest, my stomach, my hips. The anticipation is killing
me. He finally pushes his fingers inside me and I buck my
hips up, seeking his mouth. He chuckles darkly in response.
"So greedy. Not yet, beautiful. I want to take my time."

After getting me agonizingly close, he moves away from
me. I whine in protest, "Dylan, please." I hear his belt
buckle, followed by a zipper.

"I promise I won't enter you bare, and we should have
talked about this the other night, but I need to know:
When was the last time you were tested, baby?"

I think for a moment. "About a year ago, and haven't been
with anyone since. I'm clear and also on the pill."

"I was three months ago, I'm also clear. Just want to be
sure we are both safe before I—" He finishes the sentence
by rubbing my clit with the head of his cock. Every very
few circles, he tests my entrance but doesn't push in.
Over… and over… and over. The sensation is too much;
my hands tightly grip the comforter to ground myself.
"How are you feeling, beautiful?"

I answer truthfully and breathlessly, "I need to come."

Dylan kisses me and rubs his entire length against my clit,
giving me the pressure I've been seeking. Nipping at my lip
as he breaks the kiss, he whispers, "Not yet. How do you
want to come, Emma? On my hands, my mouth, or my
cock?"

I love when he says my name, more than the nickname for
me. It's possessive and sexual. *What happened to this man in the
last decade?*

"All of them."

Falling beside me, he chuckles, pulling me on top of him. I sit up, straddling him, and he reaches up to take off my blindfold. I squint at the sudden bright light. Once my vision adjusts, I glance down at him. "Hey there, beautiful," he sighs as he lays back down. "I need you to come up here." He grips my hips to pull them toward his head. The darkness in his eyes is back to drive me crazy—or perhaps it was there this whole time? A girl can dream.

"Dylan, I'm not going to sit on your face. I'm not in my twenties anymore; I'll suffocate you with my thighs," I laugh.

"No, you won't, but if you did, I would die a happy man." He keeps tugging on my hips, as he shimmies between my legs down the bed.

He can't honestly want me to do this.

"You're going to ride my face, baby. Fuck my mouth until you come harder than you ever have in your life." *Okay, maybe he does?* I'm hovering just above his mouth nervously when he demands, "I said sit, E. Hands on the headboard if you need leverage, but I need to taste you."

He pulls my hips down, forcing me onto his mouth, sucking hard on my clit. I cry out as I rock against his mouth. His tongue keeps a steady pressure and two of his fingers enter me, pressing against me where I need him. I was so close before when he was teasing me. As he adds a third, it takes me over the edge instantly, my orgasm barreling through me hard and fast. My entire body feels like it's vibrating, my walls pulsing around his fingers.

"Attagirl. I fucking love when you come on my tongue—it's like taking a shot of honey. Fuck, give me another, baby."

I catch my breath and attempt to move off him—which, honestly, feels a lot like dismounting a horse. Dylan holds me in place. "I just need a second. That was…" I have no words. He lets me go so I can lay down on the bed. Trying to collect myself, I turn to find him propped up on his elbow, resting his head on his hand and watching me intently. This man has given me at least four orgasms this past week, and I never even touched him. I know he said it doesn't matter, but to me it does. I want to see him come undone.

My insecurities seep in that I'm not enough and once he has me, he'll disappear again. I take a deep breath and mirror him, and he reaches out to grab my hip, pulling me closer. I look between us and he's so painfully hard, a little precum glistens on the tip. I reach to feel him, but he grabs my wrist and his eyes darken. "I meant what I said the other night, I'm not coming in your hand."

"Fine." I move down the bed until I am nearly eye level with his cock. "You never said anything about my mouth." Before he can protest again, I swipe my tongue from base to his tip, then take him deep, gagging lightly.

"Fuck." He thrusts his hips up in response and the loss of control makes me feel powerful—I love that I can drive him as crazy as he drives me. His cock is heavy on my tongue as I gently tugs on his balls. After moving up and down his shaft several times, he tightens up, already close. I'm not surprised; he's been hard for nearly an hour.

I love listening to his groans while I fuck him with my mouth. Just when I think he's almost there, he stops me and wraps my hair around his fist as he pulls me off him. Shaking his head, he's breathless as he demands, "No, baby, not your mouth either. But damn, *fuck*, that felt incredible." He slides me up his body, bringing me in for a bruising kiss, then leans over to reach in his bag at the end of the bed, pulling out a condom. "Is this still okay? As much as I want to be inside you, you can say no at any point."

"Yes." I expect him to roll on the condom, but he pauses. A crease forms between his eyebrows as anguish etches his eyes. I reach up and brush my thumb over his frown and ask softly, "Dylan, are you okay?"

He shakes his head, his expression almost pained. "I'm just afraid if we do this, that I'll have moved too fast, and I'll lose you for good."

I ponder it for a moment, knowing there's a very good chance that he's right. This man has professed his love for me and selflessly pulled orgasm after orgasm out of me, and I've given him nothing in return—emotionally or physically. There's a real possibility that if we have sex tonight, he could be the last man I ever sleep with. It terrifies me. We only started to get to know each other again.

I move to sit next to him, and he takes my hand in his, placing it on his heart like he did the other night. "You're right," I admit. "I'm not where you're at emotionally, because a part of me is still so worried you're going to hurt me again. But I promise you that, unless that happens, I won't be going anywhere. We just need to take this one step at a time and not rush into something too emotionally heavy."

His expression remains unreadable, and I dare to continue, "I was *so* in love with you, but that was years ago. I want to get to know who you are *now*. And that's hard to do when you're giving me multiple orgasms." He chuckles, then cups my cheek to pull me in for a brief kiss—the same sweet and gentle kiss he gave me so many years ago.

My heart aches. He's ready for us to pick up where we left off and live some happily ever after from movies and books. I brush his hair off his forehead. "Dylan, we aren't kids anymore. There are so many variables now. If we are going to do this—you and me—maybe you're right and we should probably hit pause on the physical stuff this week-end." He leans his forehead to mine. "I don't mind fooling around a little." I groan at my choice of words. "Gah, I sound like some old lady! But maybe we shouldn't have sex this weekend."

Dylan laughs at my self-deprecating humor, then sighs, "I admit, I tend to get carried away when we're together, but you and I both know I want more than that. I love—" He clears his throat. "I lost you once, I don't want to lose you again by taking things too far, too fast. I hope you don't think this weekend was to get in your pants."

"I don't think that's why we're here." I huff a small laugh. "But if we didn't discuss this, I'm sure we wouldn't leave this bed for the rest of the weekend. The other day, you said you struggle with taking things slow. Well, I do too. There's always been this pull between us that I never could explain, but we should probably slow down. I want to be honest with you. This scares me, but only because I don't want to rush things and have it blow up in our faces."

Dylan's smile gives me all the reassurance I need that I've made the right choice in us setting this boundary. He stands, offering me his hand. "It's not going to blow up in our faces. I won't let it. Come on, beautiful, let's get cleaned up and get you to bed." Leading me to the bathroom, he turns on the shower, and glances over his shoulder at me. "I hope you know, you're truly the most incredible woman I have ever known. I'm yours, even if you're not mine again."

How can I not fall for this man when he says things like that to me?

Guiding us both into the shower, he pulls me in close, every inch of us touching. I'm the biggest hypocrite in the world as I reach between us. I want to touch him, feel the weight of him in my hand, take him in my mouth again, to have him come on my chest... moaning *my* name. Just as my fingers graze the head of his cock, he stops me, grabbing my wrist. "Emma, I warned you. When we do this, I won't be coming here"—he kisses my fingertips, then the pad of his thumb grazes my bottom lip—"or here." He kisses me, his hands moving to my lower back, pulling me impossibly closer to him, then he slides down my body until he is on his knees.

"What are you doing?"

He lifts one of my legs over his shoulder; I brace myself with the shower wall. "I told you I want one more from you, baby."

I run my hands through his hair, and protest, "But what about—" His tongue swirls around my clit, causing me to nearly lose my balance. He's stroking himself at the same pace he's licking and sucking. Since he refuses to let me touch him, between my moans I manage, "Dylan, will you come with me?"

He stops for just a moment, smiling up at me. "Abso-*fucking*-lutely."

I laugh at him referencing my favorite show he teased me about when we were younger. My giggles are cut short when his tongue finds my center again, and I can hardly stand. I know he's close when he picks up the pace of his mouth and hand. "Yes, right there. I'm close! I just need —" He presses two fingers deep inside me, and in seconds, I shatter. My entire body spasms and my vision blurs. I'm not even sure what year it is, and am questioning my own name.

Dylan comes with me, stifling his moan with a bite to my thigh. "That's my girl, you're fucking mine." He growls it like some kind of possessive fae high lord, bringing me back to the present.

As we catch our breaths, he stands and I wrap my arms around his neck, bringing him in to kiss me. I can taste myself on his tongue as we stand in the shower making out like a couple of horny teenagers. When he pulls back, I'm lost in his dark blue eyes, and as much as it scares me, I think he's right; I *am* his.

We get cleaned up and he wraps me in one of the fluffy robes we found in the closet. I make my way into the living room for a moment and grab my suitcase, bringing it back into the bedroom to pull out my toiletry bag. Standing next to each other in front of the dual sink brushing our teeth, it feels comfortable, as if we've been doing this every night for years. If he hadn't disappeared, maybe this would've been an anniversary trip.

Leaning over my suitcase on the bed, I'm about to pull out my pajamas when Dylan sneaks up behind me and wraps his arms around my waist. His lips find that sensitive spot between my neck and shoulder, and I can't help melting into him.

"Hey, beautiful. I don't mind if you want to sleep naked."

I consider it for a moment. Turning in his arms to face him, I shake my head. "I'm pretty sure if I sleep naked, we won't leave this room for the rest of the trip."

"You're right. But even with clothes on, you know I won't be able to keep my hands off you."

I change into my silk pajamas and he puts on a pair of boxer briefs. I catch a glimpse of his beautiful almost-naked body. *Does this man have zero percent body fat?* He picks up his phone and retrieves a blanket from the closet.

As he makes his way to the bedroom door, I grab his hand to stop him. "What are you doing?"

"I just need to set up everything in the other room. I'll stay with you until you fall asleep, but I'm sleeping on the couch." There isn't a hint of teasing. He squeezes my hand three times before he continues, "I promised you two rooms, E."

"No. Stay with me." *Does he not want to?*

Dylan pauses for a moment. "Are you sure? I can sleep on the couch, I don't mind. I'm a man of my word... Well, I at least try to be. When it comes to you, all bets are off."

"Yes." I kiss his cheek. "Now, come on. I'm tired and, if I don't get at least six hours, I'm going to be cranky tomorrow."

We slide into bed and plug in our phones to charge. After turning off the light on the bedside table, he pulls me to him, my back flush with his firm chest. He softly kisses my shoulder—my new favorite place for him to kiss me—and whispers, "Thank you for coming this weekend."

I smile and reply quietly into the darkness, "Thank you for this weekend. Goodnight, Dylan."

"Night, beautiful."

We fall asleep quickly; I'm exhausted from all of the non-sex sex we had tonight. A few hours later, my phone lights up. Ever since having the kids, I've been a light sleeper, and the brightness of the phone is enough to trigger my fight or flight response. Worried it's the kids, I swiftly lift my phone to look at it.

ETHAN

Hey, sexy lady! Miss you! Can we get together next week for drinks?

Sure, how's Tuesday? O'Brian's?

Works for me. Have a good night, gorgeous. Don't do anything I would do.

I chuckle to myself and close my messages. After putting my phone on *do not disturb*, I fall back asleep, still wrapped in Dylan's arms.

17

EMMA

Rolling over, I reach for Dylan. The bed is warm but empty. I glance at my phone on the bedside table—10:43 a.m.. *Holy crap!* I never sleep in this late, even when I don't have the kids. I get up, pad off to the bathroom to brush my teeth, and pull out my tinted moisturizer. *Screw it, I am not wearing real makeup today.*

After I get dressed, I wander into the main space, looking for Dylan. He's sitting on the couch with his ankle resting on the opposite knee, reading something on one of the ereaders. Wearing a black tee and gray sweatpants—*fuck, he wore his glasses, too*—the whole look is a lethal combination. I didn't want to disturb him, but he hears me come in anyway.

"Hey, beautiful, hope I didn't wake you."

He moves to stand, but I gesture for him to stop. "Don't get up. You didn't wake me, I'm going to grab a cup of coffee and I'll come join you."

Disregarding my request, he continues to get up and makes his way to me. He tucks a rogue strand of hair behind my ear and insists, "I'll grab it, sit down and relax. I ran up to the main cabin and grabbed oat milk creamer for you, too." He presses a gentle kiss to my lips and moves past me to the kitchen.

I take a seat and spot both ereaders on the coffee table, picking up the one that's currently off. Once powered on, I'm impressed to find a variety of books—mystery, romance, fantasy, and a few biographies. I drape a blanket over my legs and make myself comfortable before downloading the sequel to a romantasy series I've been meaning to read.

Dylan returns, handing me a cup of coffee as he sits next to me. After pulling half of my blanket over his legs, he makes himself comfortable, resting his arm on the back of the couch behind me.

I'm combing through the front matter when he sneaks a peek at what I'm reading. "So, what's this one about?"

"There's an author that I am obsessed with, Marianne A. Scott. Her new book came out that's part of her fantasy series. It's about a witch who meets this prince, and you think he is the one, but I don't think he's endgame. I'm rooting for the wolf guy."

His eyes widen. "I didn't know you read fantasy books."

"Well, it's no *Game of Thrones* or *Harry Potter*. It's more of a romance and there's a lot more, um… sex in it." I don't know why I'm so embarrassed; he's had his face between my legs.

A sly smile creeps across his face. "Maybe I should read it with you."

"Okay." I grab his ereader from him. "But you have to read the first one to get what's happening." I download the first book on his device and hand it back to him. "All set."

Dylan lowers his arm to wrap around me, pulling me closer to him as he kisses the top of my head. "Thanks."

We sit quietly, reading for a few hours, but I check in every so often to see what part of the book he's at. My stomach grumbles and, no matter how I try to hide it, he notices. "Hey, baby, are you hungry? We didn't have breakfast, or even lunch. I lost track of time."

"Sure, we should probably eat something." He sets both of our devices down on the coffee table, then takes our mugs and places them in the sink.

He looks back at me. "Hey, come here."

I join him in the kitchen and he wraps me in a tight hug. Letting out a sigh of contentment, he kisses my temple. "Thanks again for coming. The last few weeks have been busy with work and the girls. I really needed to get away."

"Of course, I get it. Sometimes you need a few days to recharge the batteries." With a soft smile, he leans in to kiss me. Being with him is easy, and part of me enjoys how effortlessly we are falling back into a relationship—or whatever this is.

After putting on our shoes and jackets, we head out on the path to the main cabin to grab a quick lunch. We talk about work, our kids, and friends. I haven't asked about his ex and he hasn't asked about mine. I know a little from what Lily told me and am worried it will be a heavy conversation. Right now, I don't want heavy, I need easy. He suggests we take a walk around the lake, and while I could totally stay inside all day, I jump at the opportunity to stretch my legs.

Coffee in hand, we stroll along the perimeter. He hasn't stopped touching me since I woke up this morning—his arm consistently around my shoulders, or holding my hand.

Is this what it'll be like when we go back to reality?

It all feels eerily familiar to the last time, when we'd attend each other's work and family events. He was always so proud to show everyone I was his, even if I was self-conscious about how he was the attractive one between the two of us. It's been in the back of my mind: What happened? He says he was young and dumb but there has to be more to it. Maybe I'm just overthinking it.

After an afternoon exploring the lake and a quick trip to the grocery store, we head back to the cabin. As I finish putting the perishables away, he comes up behind me, swiftly pulling me against him. He murmurs into my hair, "I'm going to hop in the shower really quick, then I'll start dinner."

I turn to face him, my palms on his chest. "Hey now, I am more than capable of starting dinner."

"I know, but sit down and relax. Let me take care of it."

I lift onto my toes to kiss him. My ex-husband and I always took turns making meals, and ever since the divorce, it's been difficult balancing work and home life. A man offering to cook? He doesn't have to tell me twice.

What starts as sweet quickly becomes hot and deliciously consuming. His hand tangles in my hair, tugging slightly to tilt my head back. As he kisses along my jaw to my neck, I wrap my arms behind him to bring him closer. He nips at me in response, making me chuckle.

I pull back slightly to tell him, "You should probably go shower, or we'll never have dinner." He gives me one last peck to my lips before pulling away completely, and surprises me when his hand smacks my ass, and I yelp, "Hey!"

Smirking, that damn dimple appears as he replies, "Sit your sexy ass down on that couch. I'll be out in a minute."

I make my way over to the couch to pick up where I left off in my book. A few minutes later, Dylan calls my name from the bedroom. I set down my book, and make my way into the other room. As I get closer, I only hear the shower. The bathroom door is slightly ajar. I knock twice…

And that's when I hear him.

"Fuck, you feel so good… That's it… Just like that… Such a good fucking girl, taking me so well."

Oh. My. God. He's jerking off.

Curiosity gets the best of me, and I open the door slightly, peering in. I can't see much of him through the steam in the shower, but he has one hand on the wall in front of him and the other stroking his thick length up and down.

"Fuck yes, baby, just like that… come for me, beautiful."

Shit, shit, shit! I should not be watching him.

I turn quickly, and as I am about to close the door, his

voice stops me. "Like what you see?" He's staring right at me with darkened eyes.

I suck in a breath. "I, uh, I'm sorry. I heard my name and thought you needed something... I'll go. I'm sorry, I didn't mean to, um..." I can't seem to collect my thoughts or words. Mostly, I'm unable to look away from his glistening, chiseled body.

"I'm not embarrassed." He opens the door an inch wider, the outline of his hand still on his cock working long, slow strokes is more apparent. I shouldn't be staring, but with him doing this, thinking of me, has me so turned on. I can't help it.

"I'm not embarrassed, either. I just, um..." My cheeks are hot. I should leave, but my legs refuse to move.

"I'm sorry." His hand stops stroking. "I don't want you to feel uncomfortable."

I find my voice and raise my chin in indignation. "I'm not. Uncomfortable, that is. Keep going."

His eyes widen in surprise for just a moment before they soften. He licks his lips, where his trademark smirk makes an appearance. I take a step toward the shower as he continues slowly pumping his hand up and down his cock.

"Tell me what you were thinking about before I walked in."

The lust hasn't left his eyes. "I was thinking about how amazing it will be to have you beneath me again, to feel your tight pussy gripping my cock as you come."

I take another step. "What else?" I take off my sweater and toss it on the ground, followed by my bra.

"Fuck, Emma, how can I think when you're standing there topless? Do you not see what you do to me?"

Of course, I know *exactly* what I'm doing—I want him to lose control. I slip out of my pants slowly, giving him a show. "Do you know how turned on I am watching *you*, knowing you were thinking of me while you fucked your hand?"

Fully naked and taking one last step toward the shower, I place my hand on the glass. Without breaking eye contact, my other hand grazes my stomach, moving lower until my fingers are between my legs. I tease my clit with slow, tortured circles. With our eyes locked, he comes hard and quick, my name on his lips. My lips part as his cum paints the shower wall.

Dylan flings open the door, and snatches a towel off the hook, wiping his face and tossing it on the ground quickly. Without drying off the rest of his body, he reaches for me, wrenching me against his hard, wet chest.

My arms instinctively move up and around his neck. "Dylan, you're getting me all wet!" He reaches down, grabs my legs behind my thighs and lifts me in one swift motion. I hook them around his waist, closing the distance and I can't help kissing him.

Carrying me into the bedroom, his lips never leaving mine. Before he sets me down on the bed, he whispers, "Do you have any idea how hot that was? You think you're wet now, just wait until I'm done with you."

18

DYLAN

When Emma undressed in the bathroom and began touching herself, it took everything in me not to drag her into the shower and take her right there. It had to be the hottest thing I've ever experienced in, well, ever. I was already close when she walked in, but watching her play with herself did me in. She never would've done that when we were younger, and I am loving this unexpected side of her.

This weekend away with her confirmed for me that she was always the woman I was meant to be with—I knew it from the moment I saw her, all those years ago. It has nothing to do with how sexually attracted to her I am, and everything to do with how vivacious she is. It scared the shit out of me when we were younger.

When I'm with Emma, she is my world. I was so drawn to her, still am, if not exponentially more than years ago. She reeled me in with her ambition, warmth, and confidence. We both had huge goals, which was something I rarely found in women in their twenties. She knew what she wanted, and went for it in every aspect of her life.

Years later, that hasn't changed. But she's harder, more cautious. She's been hurt and I know I'm partially to blame for that... if not completely to blame. I was so incredibly stupid, thinking if I could land Emma, I should play the field to make sure she really was the one. The joke was on me, because I never found anyone who ever compared to her. For years, I thought she was gone for good.

But she's mine again.

I don't know what happened with her ex, but he made a mistake in letting her go. I am not about to make the same mistake myself again, and I'll do anything in my power to make this woman happy. She makes me feel like I'm the only person in the room, breathing belief into me, and making me feel as if I can take on the world.

She's home.

Did I make sure she came twice for me before dinner? Hell yes, I did. But I'm just getting started; I don't just want her body, I want all of her.

Laying on the bed, barely able to move, she asks if I can find her something to wear. I rummage in her suitcase in search of comfortable clothes, spotting and holding up the leggings she was going to wear yesterday.

"Seriously? You're going to be the death of me."

She smirks, then snatches them from my hand. "Want me to give your eulogy?"

"You expect me to make dinner, and not skip to dessert? Especially after that little stunt you pulled in the bathroom?"

Emma puts on her leggings, and it isn't lost on me that she has no underwear underneath. I toss her a shirt that she puts on without a bra.

Nope, there's absolutely no way I'm going to be able to keep my hands off her while making dinner.

I need to slow things down. As much as I love touching her, I want more. I'm not going to keep Emma if I scare her off by moving too fast.

Once we are both dressed, I lead her into the kitchen and we pull out the ingredients for salad and spaghetti bolognese. Cooking together feels as if this is the way things were always supposed to be. I can imagine coming home from work each day, then spending time in our kitchen together, making dinner for all our kids. The daydream warms my chest and I can't help but smile.

"Hey, what are you smiling about over there?"

Damn, she caught me.

"Nothing… Well, that's a lie." I make my way over to her chopping vegetables and wrap my arms around her from behind. "I just feel like we're in our own little world here, and I'm not ready to go back to reality tomorrow." It's the closest version of the truth I'll ever come up with.

Emma sets everything down and turns in my arms. "You know, reality is what we make it. If you want this, then we'll need to work for it."

"Do you want this?" The question makes me feel vulnerable. *Would she say no?*

"Who wouldn't want to spend their evenings like this?" She shrugs, then looks away from me.

The non-answer has me pressing again; I need to know. "What do you want, E? What does our life look like when we leave here?"

Her sparkling blue eyes find mine, searching for her answer. "I don't know, but we'll take it day by day, and figure it out together."

I lean in and press my lips to her temple, wrapping my arms tighter. "Damn, I love you."

Shit! Do I take it back? Do I correct myself?

Emma freezes in my arms and I clear my throat. "I'm sorry, that kind of just slipped out."

There's a little concern, but her eyes are otherwise soft. "It's okay, today was pretty perfect, wasn't it?"

"Yeah, it really was."

She playfully pushes me toward the stove. "Okay, Romeo, keep an eye on the sauce, or we'll be ordering take out tonight." Returning to her chopping, she's still smiling, stealing glances every so often. I didn't blow it. I know she still loves me, I just need to prove she can trust me.

After dinner, we make ourselves comfortable on the couch in front of the fireplace. She's cuddled up next to me, reading her new fantasy book on her ereader. I'm nearly done with the first book in the series she's reading, then I'll be diving into a biography I started last week.

I don't want today to end; being away from reality, I can pretend she's always been mine.

After finishing a few chapters, Emma turns to face me. "Can I be honest about something?"

"Of course, I hope you can always be honest with me." I do my best to keep my expression neutral, even if the question makes me nervous.

She takes a deep breath. "We haven't talked about either of our past relationships, and I don't want to pry. *Well...* yes I do. I know you were married and want to know what happened."

I didn't expect it, but I should have. We really should have discussed it sooner. I shift nervously and rub my hands on my thighs. "There's no nice way of saying this. Ashley left us; me and my girls. We were young when we got married. She was only the second person I dated after you, and we only got married because she was pregnant with Harriet. You asked me why I named her after the character... I was still so in love with you, and wanted a piece of you to stay with me. Ashley never knew. She loved the name—and Elizabeth—so that's what we went with for the girls. I grew to love her over the years, but in the last six or so, things were just sort of routine. We became more roommates than spouses."

Emma places her hand in mine, sensing how uneasy I am talking about this. The only other person I've ever told everything to is Andrew, and the pain is still raw. "One day, while at work, I was served papers. I came home to find half of everything we owned gone. Luckily, she left all of the girls' stuff. She moved to Paris a week later with some guy from work, and we haven't seen her since. It's just the three of us now."

There's so much sadness in Emma's eyes when she replies, "I'm so sorry, that's awful."

I don't know how her own marriage ended; Andrew never told me. Unable to help myself, I ask, "What happened with your husband?"

She looks away, as if in thought. "Jason was a good man— *is* a good man. It just wasn't meant to be. It was probably my fault it ended. I was in denial for so long that Aiden is autistic, that when he was diagnosed, my extra time was devoted to him and the twins. I felt as if I needed to make up for my failing them, when in reality, he was born beautifully different and I should've embraced it. My boys were my focus, and I didn't put a lot of effort into my marriage. Then, I was promoted to VP, so between work and the boys, I never really made time for Jason. The divorce was civil, and honestly, we're both happier apart than we were together. I know it's weird, but we're good friends now, and I'm thankful to have a strong relationship with him."

We both sit in silence for a moment before she continues, "He's a great dad, but… he didn't love me anymore. If I'm being completely honest, it was mutual. I made mistakes, I didn't make him a priority. He played minor league baseball, even got called up to the majors for a moment, but got injured a few months after we got married. Then, he took a job as a college athletics director. He's an amazing coach, but I don't think it fills his cup the same way, you know? I should have done more to support him, even if he wasn't in love with me anymore. I can't blame him for not being in love with me, I never loved him the way—"

She doesn't finish the sentence but I know how it ends. My chest aches hearing it—how on earth could someone not love my Emma? *My* Emma.

I continue to listen as she shifts to get comfortable. "It's why I'm worried about things moving so fast with you. Part of me has always questioned if I've ever been enough for someone. I either give too much or too little. I married him because it was easy, but I don't think I ever gave him my whole heart. The last time I did…" She pauses again and I know how that sentence ends too. "I'm afraid now and keep everyone at arm's length, so I don't get hurt."

This is my fault. All of it. I loved her—*still love her*—but because of me, she hasn't truly loved anyone else.

This ends now.

"Emma, I'm going to say something, and I need you to really hear it. You are incredible; you always have been. The fact that I could've ever made you feel less than that… I promise I'll do everything in my power to make it up to you each and every day, to prove that you're all I want—all that I ever wanted."

A single tear leaves her eye and I wipe it away with the pad of my thumb. She lets out a deep breath, then says with a soft chuckle, "Well, that got heavy."

My lips tilt up. "Yeah, yeah it did. But I'm glad we can talk about this, and be honest with one another." I kiss her cheek where the tear fell. "I'm not taking it back, I meant what I said. I do love you. And before you say anything, I know you're not there yet, but I will spend the rest of my life showing you how much you've always meant to me."

Emma wraps her arms around me. "Thank you for letting me take my time and not forcing me to rush into this, even if it feels like we are. I want you to know that I don't take it lightly. I promise I'll always tell you what I'm thinking. I don't want to hurt you. And for what it's worth, I hope you know I really do care about you. I never stopped, no matter how much I tried." She pulls back, takes a deep breath, then shifts to get up. "I'm going to put the kettle on for a cup of tea, would you like one?"

I offer my hand to help her get up, but don't let go. Instead, I kiss her knuckles. "Sure, whatever you make, I'll drink."

We talk until well after midnight. Emma shares hilarious stories about her kids and I tell her about life as a girl-dad, since she never got to experience it. When she lets out a yawn, I'm saddened to hear her ask, "Mind if I go to bed?"

I don't want this to end, but nod. "Sure, beautiful, it's getting late. We have to get up early to beat traffic down the mountain." I take our mugs to the kitchen and place them in the sink while she heads off to the bedroom.

After I turn off all of the lights, I walk in to find she's already under the covers, almost asleep. "E, are you still awake?"

She sighs, and says something unintelligible, so I crawl into bed with her, holding her close.

I don't ever want to let her go.

19

EMMA

I wake up wrapped in Dylan's arms, not wanting this weekend to. More importantly, I don't want to pop the bubble we've been living in for the last day and a half. I must have stirred him, because he pulls me closer, kissing my shoulder.

"Good morning, beautiful."

"Good morning. I don't want to get up."

I can't help my wide smile as I feel his laughter against my back. "Me either, but if we don't, we're going to get stuck in traffic, and I need to get back to my girls tonight."

It dawns on me, I didn't get a single call all weekend. I jolt upright to check my phone and it's still on *do not disturb*. I swear under my breath as I open my phone to switch it over, finding four missed calls from Riley, twelve missed calls from Lily, at least three dozen emails, and a text from Ethan. Thankfully, nothing about the kids. My heart rate slows.

I open my texts first and chuckle at a meme Ethan sent me about how he needs to read his TBR books, instead of buying new ones.

Dylan's low rumble startles me from my message. "What's so funny?"

"Just this meme my friend sent me." Turning my phone to show Dylan the image, he huffs a small laugh. I text Lily and Riley to let them know all is well, and promise I'll debrief them when I get home.

Dylan and I get dressed, tidy up the cabin, and pack our bags to leave. I hate saying goodbye to this place. It was the perfect weekend, and now we have to go back to our lives with work and children.

On the drive home, the silence is deafening, so I ask if I can listen to my audiobook. He nods and I plug in my phone to stream it through the speakers.

We're almost home when his phone vibrates with a call. "Hey, mind if I plug in? I'll need to take this." I nod and unplug my phone for him to use it and he takes the call. "This is Dylan."

"Sorry to bother you on the weekend, we just need to be sure you'll have an answer for us by tomorrow." The man on the other end of the phone sounds older, maybe in his sixties, and no nonsense.

"Yes, Norm, I am aware of the deadline. I promise I'll have my answer by tomorrow."

It's been a while since I've seen Dylan in a professional capacity. I don't want to pry. *What am I saying? Of course I want to pry!* I know it's none of my business, but I'm curious what this cryptic conversation is about.

"Thank you, we'll chat tomorrow." The man hangs up and Dylan blows out a long breath.

"Everything okay?"

Dylan briefly glances at me before returning his eyes to the road. "Yeah, they just want me to take over the main office."

"That's amazing!" I place my hand on his leg. "Why aren't you more excited about this?"

He takes my hand and brings my knuckles to his lips before resting our joined hands back on his thigh, not letting go. "I don't think that's what I want anymore."

"It sounds like a good opportunity. What's the plan, if you don't take over the office?" He squeezes my hand three times. "Dylan, that isn't an answer."

"I'm thinking of the big picture. I want to be able to work from home, so I can be there for our—*my* kids." He clears his throat. "My kids. I want to work from home for... *Oh, fuck it*. Yeah, I slipped up there." He pulls off the highway.

"Why are we stopping? We're only fifteen minutes from home." I don't really want to have a serious conversation about this in his car. It feels rushed.

"I want to talk about this."

Damn it.

"Okay," I say carefully. "What do you want to talk about?"

"This, you and me. I'm thinking long term, E. Fuck, if you suggested we run off to Vegas right now, I would do it. I want to make plans that include you and your boys. If I take this position, it means long hours, and I won't be around as much as I want to. I want to work from home so I can have more time with you."

Well, shit.

I take a deep breath. "Answer me this: If I wasn't in the picture, would you take over the office?"

He ponders for a moment before answering. "I don't know. Part of me wonders if I would be any good at it."

"Are you serious? You would be perfect for it; they would be lucky to have you. But only do it if you want to. You're too valuable to be wasting away years working a job you hate." I omit that I don't want him to miss out on this opportunity because of me.

"I don't want it. There are more important things in my life than taking on more work responsibilities. I don't need the money, so what's the point? I don't know. You think I should take it?"

"That's not what I'm saying. If you want it, do it. If you don't, then don't. Just be sure it's for the right reasons. Which should *not* be—"

"Let me guess. You? I can't think of a better reason."

"This, whatever this is, is new. What if things don't work out and you miss a chance at something you wanted?" He's not getting it.

Dylan answers in a way I should have expected, but didn't —he leans in and kisses me softly. I melt into him, even though it's not the rational option. When he pulls back, his sexy dimples are back where they belong.

Wait, no, I'm mad at him!

"E, you're adorable."

"Adorable? I am a lot of things, adorable isn't one of them." I cross my arms over my chest.

"I'm not taking the job, but the fact that you think I could means a lot."

I sigh, knowing he won't budge on this, at least not right now. "We can talk more about this later. Come on, let's get home." He pulls me in, bringing his lips to mine again, but I pull away, no matter how much I don't want to. "Dylan, we can't just make out in your car all morning."

"Are you sure?" He winks before taking my hand and driving back onto the highway.

The last fifteen or so minutes back to my house are quiet. When we arrive, he gathers my bag from the trunk, and walks me inside. As soon as I enter, the air changes between us. It's heavy and I don't like it.

Once he sets down my bag, I wrap my arms around his middle. He kisses me softly, but I don't want his gentle kisses. I want him to take what he wants like he did at the cabin. As if he can sense it, he deepens our kiss, our tongues fighting for dominance as he pushes me up against the wall. He's kissing me like this is our last, but this isn't goodbye... At least I hope not.

"Dylan?" Anxiety bubbling up inside me, I pull back and try to assess why his kisses feel desperate. "Dylan, wait. What's wrong?"

There is so much sadness in his eyes when he replies, "I just had the most amazing weekend with the most extraordinary woman I've ever known. Now, I have to go back to life and responsibilities, without you." With a small smile, he continues jokingly, "Quick! Let's get back in the car and go back."

I can't help but laugh at the faux impulsivity. "Nothing has to change." My eyes search his, feeling the need to reassure him. "I mean, sure, life is crazy with our jobs and kids, but I want to make this work. After this weekend, I feel like I am ready for… whatever this is."

He peppers slow soft kisses on my cheek, my neck, then back up to my lips. "When can I see you again?"

Incredibly turned on from having his mouth on me, I need a moment to think before answering. "I, uh, I'm meeting my friend for drinks on Tuesday, so maybe Wednesday, if I can get a sitter?"

He groans into my neck. "It's going to be the longest three days of my life."

"Yes, but absence makes the heart grow fonder."

I didn't want to let her go. If I didn't have to pick up the girls from my parents, I would've asked to stay the night, just to remain blissfully wrapped in our little bubble for a little longer. After the weekend we had, I can't imagine a single moment without her.

The last two days have been a blur. Work piled up—probably in retaliation from my decision to not take the job—and I haven't had a chance to talk to or text Emma, other than good morning or good night. We made plans for tomorrow night, which can't come soon enough.

Eating lunch at my desk, I'm about to message her when I get a call from Andrew. The moment I pick up, he launches in, "Hey man, how was your weekend away?" I'm thankful that he isn't still hung up on my dating his and Lily's friend.

"It was fucking amazing! I really needed to get away. Are we still on for tonight?"

"Of course, how about O'Brians? The game should be on."

"Sure, I'll meet you there around six." We hang up and the rest of the day is a grind so I can leave in time to meet him.

When I arrive, the pub is packed and our usual booth is taken. Opting to sit at the bar, he orders an IPA and I order my usual gin and tonic, but with extra lime. I don't normally order it that way, but it reminds me of Emma. It's barely been forty-eight hours—forty-eight hours too long.

The drink is almost to my lips when I hear Emma's laugh. I shake my head. It's not possible, I'm a lovestruck fool imagining things. I take a few sips and hear it again. After a quick scan of the room, I spot her sitting in a booth with a man's arm draped behind her. I almost spit out my drink.

No, it can't be her. She said she was hanging out with a friend tonight. Did she blow me off for a date?

Andrew follows my line of sight. "Oh, hey! Your girl is here." It doesn't seem to faze him that she's with another man, instead takes a long drink of his beer and continues, "I gotta take a leak, but when I come back, let's go say hi."

All I see is red. She was so hesitant to date me, but she is out with *this guy?* He looks like a fucking Ken doll; he can't be her type. I don't wait for Andrew, and cross the room to confront her.

As I approach their table, there's no denying she's definitely on a date. From the looks of it, this isn't their first. She doesn't look up, until I address her. "Hey, E." My voice is a little clipped, but what does she expect? She's on a fucking date after the weekend we just had. I know we never talked about being exclusive, but it felt implied.

Emma's eyes are wide with surprise, but not like she just got caught on a date. "Hey! What are you doing here?" She looks genuinely happy to see me, which is unexpected.

Maybe I read this wrong?

"Have you met Ethan? He's also friends with Andrew, so maybe you've met before?"

"No, I can't say that I have. Hi, I'm Dylan." *Do I add 'her boyfriend?'*

"Hey, man." He reaches out to shake my hand, but his other arm is still wrapped around her. "I'm Ethan. I've heard *so much* about you." He doesn't like what he's heard about me. What did she tell him?

Emma clears her throat. "Right, well, Ethan and I are catching up. Can I call you later when I get home?"

Fuck, is she brushing me off?

I glance behind me to the bar; Andrew is nowhere to be found. As I turn back, Emma's checking her buzzing phone. "Shoot, sorry guys, one sec. I need to take this." She slides out of the booth, squeezing my bicep as she passes me, but doesn't address Ethan. *Interesting.* I slide in to sit for a moment, I need to feel this guy out.

As soon as she's out of earshot, he leans in, lowering his voice, "So, you're the asshole who ghosted her." He clucks his tongue three times, and I defensively straighten my posture, even if he's not wrong. "What. An. Idiot. I have to ask, what were you thinking? The most incredible woman walks into your life, and you let her go? My Emma is a tough woman, but you sure did a number on her with that little disappearing act of yours."

Did he just call her 'his Emma?' What the fuck?

"What the hell do you know about it? Who the fuck are you? She's never mentioned an Ethan before." *Has she been seeing him the whole time we've been back together?*

"I know more than you can imagine. Maybe you're not that close after all. I've known her for almost twenty years. In fact"—he pauses for dramatic effect—"we were texting when you were at the game. Oh, and also this weekend when you took her to that cabin, where I'm sure you tried to get in her pants, but failed miserably. Don't worry, I know about that too. So, now that her husband is out of the picture, you think you can slide into her DMs, and sweep her off her feet like nothing happened? I was there to pick up the pieces last time, and I plan on being there again, when you fuck it up."

Heat creeps up my neck as I watch him take a long, deliberate sip of his Old Fashioned. It occurs to me that the meme friend is Ethan. She was texting *him* almost every time we were together. This is her supposed best friend, but all I see is competition.

"There won't be any pieces to pick up. She's mine now, so I suggest you back off." I don't know how Emma feels about him, but from the way he was touching her, it's clear he wants her.

A sly grin tugs at his lips as he lets out a light chuckle. "Well, maybe she just wants to see what's out there before settling down after a divorce? I don't even need to make a move, do I? She's out with me tonight, not you. Don't worry, Houdini, I'll make sure she gets home safe. Maybe I'll even stay the night for good measure."

Anger floods my veins. I'm not going to let this douchebag take my girl. "I said she's mine, asshole. Back. Off."

"What the fuck, Dylan?" Emma huffs directly behind me, and the look on Ethan's face is like the cat who ate the canary.

I turn to face her. "I don't know what you thought you heard—"

"I heard enough." She looks to Ethan. "I'm so sorry, I need to get back to the kids, can we have a rain check?"

"Of course, Em. I'll walk you to your car." He leaves fifty dollars on the table and stands, offering to shake my hand, "Well, Damon, was it? It's been fun."

I don't take it. Instead I stand, shoulder past him, and grip Emma's elbow, guiding her a few feet away from him. "We need to talk." I look back and he's leaning against the end of the booth. He's not interfering, which I appreciate, but I don't like that he's still watching.

Emma shakes out of my hold. "Get your hands off me. How dare you! What the hell are you doing? First, you threaten my friend, and now you're going all Neanderthal on me? *She's mine, asshole*… What the hell is that? I don't get it. Don't you trust me? You came into my life a few weeks ago, you agreed to take it slow, but then you lose your shit?"

"Emma, I—"

"No, I'm not done. I've known Ethan for over half my life! What was that toxic, alpha shit back there? I'm all for some role play in the bedroom. Who doesn't want to be told *this pussy is mine* in the heat of the moment? But you do *not* own me; I am not a piece of property." Her fingers find the bridge of her nose as she mutters to herself, "I already have three children, I don't need a fourth." She steps back and lets out a disappointed sigh. "We'll talk about this later, I need to get home right now. My son is in the middle of a sensory melt-down, that's what the call was. I don't know how much you know about neurodivergent people, but right now, he is my priority, not your ego. This is the *last* thing I need." I try to stop her, but she pushes me away. "Don't touch me, Dylan."

I don't follow as she leaves, my stomach twisting as Ethan wraps his arm around her.

Glancing back to Andrew at the bar, he's shaking his head. I walk over to him. "Did you enjoy the show?"

"I only caught the last bit, but you can't say I didn't warn you about her. I told you she doesn't do casual. If she's with you, she's *only* with you. I'm not sure why you lost your cool with Ethan, but seeing Emma rip into you has to be the highlight of my year." He laughs and takes a long pull of his beer. "Well, that's my cue. I need to talk to Lily before she gets wind of this whole thing. She's going to want to check in with Emma about Aiden. Drinks are on you." Andrew stands and pats me on the back, leaving me on my stool to marinate in the consequences of my actions.

I pull out my phone to call Emma, but my thumb hovers over the call button; I know she won't answer. Instead, I signal to the bartender to close out my tab.

On the drive home, I play back everything that just happened. I never lose my cool, but all bets are off when it comes to this woman. This can't be it for us; I feel it in my soul that she's it for me.

Did I just screw everything up by being a jealous asshole?

I need to talk to her, and the only way is in-person. If this is it for us, I'm not going to let her walk away in a text message.

21

EMMA

I can't believe him. We spend a great weekend together, but then he gets all jealous and possessive? It doesn't make any sense. Except—devil's advocate—Ethan is a huge flirt, and who knows what he said to Dylan.

We're almost to my car, but I stop him. "Ethan, you know I love you, right?"

His brows pinch. "Of course, you're my ride or die, babe. Even if I get married, you're always going to be my number one."

"So, tell me the truth, what did you say to Dylan to turn him into a caveman? I won't get mad, I just need to know."

"Just the truth." He chuckles. "I called him out, told him he was an idiot and that he better not screw it up."

"Ethan…" I'm using my mom voice now, even if it won't affect him.

"Okay, okay. I admit, I was *kind of* messing with him. Only a little. You know how I feel about this guy after he disappeared on you. You always thought he was the one. So I may have, sort of, kind of, perhaps a little bit, hinted that we were on a date... But not using those words. I wanted to see his reaction."

"Why would you do that? He's my boyfriend... *ish*. I don't know what we are, but I'm seeing him again. Why would you make him think I'm dating you?" I'm so confused; Ethan and I have always just been friends. You know that saying, *'he's just not that into you?'* That's Ethan, except I also don't think about him that way. From Dylan's perspective, I'm sure it looked like I'm in some weird love triangle with my best friend, but it couldn't be further from the truth.

Ethan tilts my chin, forcing me to look him in the eyes. "Emma-bear, I don't like the guy. He doesn't deserve you."

"There's a lot to unpack there. First, you have never, in our entire lives, called me Emma-bear. Please don't start now. Second, I don't care whether you like him or not. I do! You should've at least pretended to be nice, and not act like you're dating me, just to get a rise out of him." He had no business overstepping.

"I'm sorry." Ethan laughs heartily and wraps me in a tight hug. "I didn't know he was so fragile. I'll be on my best behavior from now on."

I pause for a second before responding, "I don't know if it will even be an issue anymore. If he freaks out when I go out for a drink with you, maybe he isn't the guy I thought he was."

He kisses the top of my head and he guides me by the small of my back to my car. Taking my keys out of my hand, he unlocks and opens my door for me. We say goodbye and on drive home I can't stop my inner voice, reminding me that Dylan and I don't really know each other. Not any more, at least. I get so swept up in him—old habits are hard to break. I'm lost in my thoughts when there's a new message from him.

"Play messages," I tell my hands-free system in my car.

"You have one new message from Dylan Alexander… *I'm sorry for tonight. Can I come by later?*... Would you like to reply?" I ponder it for a moment, but I need to get home to Aiden. I just hope the sitter was able to soothe him before I get there. I leave the message for later.

Once I'm home, Aiden is thankfully calm and sitting in bed, so I tuck him in. She said it took almost forty-five minutes, but when he's dysregulated, that's record time. I check on the twins and, luckily, both are in bed reading. I kiss them goodnight and make my way downstairs.

In the kitchen, I grab my favorite mug from the cupboard, and my lavender earl grey tea. I pause for a moment, staring at the box before putting it back, and take out the chamomile. *Great, he ruined tea for me.* As soon as I start the kettle, my phone vibrates on the counter and I let out a sigh. I'm a thousand percent sure it's Dylan.

He can wait.

I prepare my tea and grab my old ereader; the new one has too many memories from the weekend. I pull up a romantic suspense book by Amanda Storm I started last week, hopefully immersing myself in a book will take my mind off things.

Barely settled into one of my reading chairs, there's a soft knock at the door. *I swear to God, if it's him, I'm going to lose it.* I take out my phone to check my doorbell camera, and sure enough, there he is. I don't have the energy to deal with him, but I know he won't go away, and we should face this head on.

I quickly glance in the peephole. He's pacing, wringing his hands. I suck in a deep breath and let it out slowly before opening the door. At least I'm wearing pants this time.

"Dylan, what are you doing here?" I step outside and close the door behind me; I don't want my kids to hear this.

He stares back at me with a combination of pain and lust in his eyes. I cross my arms and wait. Finally, he breaks the silence, "I'm sorry."

He's sorry? That's it?

Resisting my urge to go to him when he looks like a wounded animal, I hold my head high. "Well, I would be sorry too if I started dating a woman, told her I loved her, had an incredible weekend giving her lots of orgasms, then lost my crap on her best friend. Even if he was trying to get under my skin." My words are practically a snarl. It's been a long night, and I'm in no mood to play games.

"Emma, I'm sorry I lost it, but you have to know how it looked!"

Wait, is he blaming me?

I lift my hands in protest. "Whoa, whoa, whoa… You're trying to pin this on *me?* I was out with a friend. Sure, he was trying to press your buttons, but you fell for it."

"E, can I please come inside, so we can talk about this?"

"What is there to talk about? I get a call from my sitter that my kid is having a rough night—you know Aiden thinks differently and has sensory differences. Well, this happens a lot when schedules or the weather change. I was already stressed out and came back to find you freaking out on Ethan. If that isn't a red flag, I don't know what is." I pause to take a deep breath. I know I'm talking fast, but I'm heated. "I know Ethan was being a dick to you. I already talked to him about it, but this isn't about him. We had an amazing weekend, but after tonight, and whatever that was... I don't know if this is going to work."

Dylan takes a step toward me, sliding his hand from my cheek and jaw, to the nape of my neck. Instead of a rebuttal, he brings me in for a hard and brutal kiss. While I absolutely love kissing this man, if I don't stop, I am sure he will strip me down right here, and this is not the time or place for me to melt into him.

My hands find his chest to push him back. "You can't solve this with something physical. No kiss or orgasm is going to fix the fact that you didn't trust me. You thought I was on a date and, instead of being an adult and asking me, you made assumptions and let a guy get in your head."

My breath is heavy. Part of me wants his mouth on me again, the other knows I need to be firm. I continue, "What's going to happen when I have a business dinner with a man? Or if I hug my best friend? Ethan only had his arm resting on the top of the booth behind me and you lost it. He overstepped when he insinuated that I was on a date, but that doesn't excuse how you acted. You thought I was with someone else before you even approached the table." I chew on my bottom lip. "Maybe this isn't the best idea right now. Maybe... Maybe we moved too fast."

Dylan cups my face, forcing me to look at him. "Emma, I know I screwed up, but you have to know that any man in my situation would've thought the same thing: That some guy was about to take his girl."

I'm done talking in circles about this. He isn't getting it, and it feels like he's trying to blame me and Ethan. I step away. I need to think of my kids right now. Can I imagine moving forward with Dylan? Marriage and him being a second father to my kids? Right now, no. Not when he's acting possessive and controlling. I couldn't handle this all the time, it's exhausting. It's one thing if it's behind closed doors or roleplaying, it's another when he is trying to control who my friends are.

"This has nothing to do with Ethan, and everything to do with you and me. You are the first and only man to really break my heart, but I gave you a second chance. I took a call that caused me to go into mom-mode, and came back to my best friend and my boyfriend bickering. You see how this looks?" He smiles at the label, so I clarify, "Yeah, I said it. It's what I thought you were after last weekend. I *wanted* to be your girlfriend because this felt real. But now? Now, I'm not so sure. Did I imagine it? Or is this just physical for you? You don't trust me."

His face falls. "Of course, I trust you! And no, it isn't just physical for me. I'm in love with you, and made the mistake of letting my jealousy take over tonight." He wraps me in a warm embrace and kisses the top of my head, murmuring into my hair, "I can't lose you again, E. I won't. You want space? Done. I'll give you space. If you want me to become best friends with Ethan? I'll be buying matching tees tomorrow." I chuckle against his chest and look up at him. "Name it, beautiful. I would give anything to fix this."

I take a deep breath. "Let's just put on the brakes for a minute. I need some time to wrap my mind around everything and focus on my kids. And I think you need to take some time to think about whether or not you can handle dating a woman who has a life outside of you, maybe get that jealousy under control. Ethan is my best friend; he's always going to be part of my life."

He reluctantly nods. "You're right. I promised I would take things at your pace, and I meant what I said when this all started, about waiting for you." He takes my hand and presses a soft kiss to my palm, then rests my hand on his cheek, his covering mine. "I screwed up tonight, please let me try to make it up to you?"

"Let's just take some time. A break. Not like a Ross and Rachel break—because we all know how that one worked out. I won't date anyone else until we figure out what this is." I step closer and kiss him softly on the cheek. He doesn't push for more, keeping his promise. As I pull away, I miss his warmth, but I need him to understand that we need to slow down. "I need to get back inside. But, are we okay?"

"I'm not going to disappear, if that's what you're hinting at. And I have no desire to date anyone else. How could I, when I'm obsessed with a fiery woman who owns my heart? I'm yours, Emma." I sigh, unable to hide my smile at his declaration. He takes my hand, kisses my knuckles, and squeezes three times before releasing it. "Can I call you tomorrow?"

I nod. "Yeah. Yes, of course."

"Goodnight, beautiful." He walks back to his car, glancing

back once, and I watch him drive off before heading inside.

22

ETHAN

I admit, I was kind of a dick. I've seen Emma through four big break-ups, including her divorce. Dylan disappeared to hook up with some other woman, without even bothering to end things with Emma first. I was there, holding her hand, convincing Emma that it wasn't her fault. She wasn't the same after—guarded, never giving her whole heart away again. Instead, she masked, playing the perfect wife or girlfriend to whoever came along after him.

Two of her other boyfriends cheated on her too, which makes absolutely no sense to me. I know, from personal experience, that Emma is amazing in bed—even if we only hooked up a couple times in college. How can you cheat on someone you can bring home to mom and dad, but once you get home, she's a freak in the sheets? I blame the books she reads, but she was always experimenting back in college, too. My girl developed a serious praise kink, and I'm worried Dylan may have picked up on it already—to say words of affirmation is her love language is an under-statement.

Her marriage began to fall apart after Aiden's diagnosis. It's not the little guy's fault, their marriage was already hanging on by a thread. The last five years or so, maybe even longer, Jason didn't put any effort in, but neither did she. They went through the motions, looking like the perfect couple on the outside, but I don't think he really ever loved her the way she deserves. She didn't love him either, so the divorce didn't destroy her. They have a great relationship now that they aren't married to each other. He's a good guy, just wasn't *the* guy.

Emma's my best friend, I'm very protective of her, especially when it comes to Dylan. I would do anything for her, and I don't want her to get hurt by the human equivalent of a participation award. If it was any other guy, I might've tried to play nice. He's not any other guy. He's her first love, the same man who broke her. I'll be damned if I let him break her again.

After last night's dumpster fire, I need to apologize. Not to the fucking unsalted pretzel of an ex-boyfriend, I need to make amends with my girl. She deserves a lot better than Dylan, who should've chosen her years ago. I take out my phone to call her, but spot a message from Lily.

> **LILY**
>
> What the hell happened last night? Emma called for an emergency buffalo plaid night. Andrew said it's because you and Dylan got into it?

> I wouldn't say we got into it. I called him out for being an idiot.

She always told me about her pajama movie nights with the girls, but I've never joined them. I need an invite and make things right with Em.

Can I come tonight? I'll even wear the matching pants!

I don't know. If Emma is okay with it, then yes. But you better be on your best behavior.

I promise. Can I bring anything? Wine?

Yes, wine! And maybe some crackers for the charcuterie board.

Got it, see you tonight! I'll get an extra pair of pj pants for your hubby too.

Oh my God, yes! You know how much he hates them. See you tonight!

I'm about to pocket my phone when there's a new message, except it isn't from Lily.

EMMA

Yes, you may join in, but only if you apologize to Dylan.

Lily moves fast! Fine, I'll apologize, but I can't help it if he doesn't like me. Not everyone has good taste.

You're impossible.

For you, I'll play nice. Give me his number and I'll call him.

Even if he is a snowflake.

Ethan...

What? He is! It took less than 60 seconds for him to snap like a twig. It was too easy!

> But fine, I'll apologize to him, if it means I can come tonight.

> Thank you.

> You're lucky I love you. I wouldn't be apologizing to mayonnaise if I didn't.

> Oh come on, he is not mayo!

> Of course he is. See you tonight!

Emma sends me his contact info. There's no time like the present to deal with the douche canoe. I cringe as I add the new contact and create a new message.

> Hey, this is Ethan. We need to talk.

> MAYO
> Yeah, we do.

> I'm free for lunch today, want to grab a burger?

> Sure. Send me an address and I'll be there at 12:30.

I send him the address for a place downtown, where I know the owner; I want to be on my own turf.

Fuck, I love this place. They serve the best grub and have karaoke on random weeknights. When I enter the bar, Dylan's already waiting for me. It's not busy, so we're seated at a booth right away.

Thank Loki! I don't want to deal with this guy any longer than necessary.

Once the host leaves us, I lay my cards on the table. "All right, look, I am just going to come out with it. I admit I was a little out of line last night, but you probably don't have the backstory." He nods for me to continue. "Emma and I have been friends since college, and I was there when you decided breaking her was a better option than wifing her up." I shake my head and I feel a surge of emotions bubbling up inside me. "And, I mean, you didn't just break her heart, you shattered it; she's never loved the same since."

His jaw tics. "I get the whole protective brother act, but things with her are still new. It really did look like she was on a date with you. I lost it. After all these years, I got her back, and I wasn't about to let her go again without a fight. I saw you as a threat." Looking off into the restaurant thoughtfully, he continues, "When we talked about our break up, she admitted that I was the only man to break her heart." He looks back at me, and there's honest concern in his eyes. "But what do you mean she never loved the same?"

"I mean just that. She always kept a part of her heart safe. There were a few serious boyfriends after you. They all cheated on her. All of them. Which just confirmed, in her mind, that she was never enough for someone. I know, I know, she's incredible. '*How could anyone do that?*' Well, they did. After them, she met Jason. He was… safe. She loved him, but I don't think she was ever *in love* with him. It was the same for him. He's a really good guy, a fucking golden retriever, but there wasn't any passion there."

I feel bad for Jason. He didn't stand a chance after this asshole broke her like the spine of a chunky paperback. Jason deserves someone who is full of life and loves with their whole heart, someone like... *Charlotte*. Too bad she's Emma's step-sister, they would've been perfect for each other.

The waitress comes by with water and takes our order. When she leaves, I take a few sips, trying to remember where I left off. I'm hit with a flashback. "I remember the night she met you. She called and told me about this guy who she had some kind of magnetic connection with, and how it was love at first sight," I sigh, shaking my head. "She was such a romantic back then. I miss that Emma."

"I felt it too. That night, I couldn't take my eyes off her. It wasn't because she was the most beautiful woman I'd ever seen—which she is—there was just something magical about her I couldn't explain. I felt so drawn to her. Still am."

Maybe he gets it?

"That's Emma though, she *is* magic. She makes you feel like you're the only other person in the whole world when you're together. I experienced it first hand, before we realized friendship was a better option for us."

"You guys dated? She's never mentioned it, even back then."

Shit, I shouldn't have said anything. That was careless. Well, too late now, here we go...

"We went out for a week or two in college when we were eighteen, but decided we were better off friends. A few years later, I moved away for a new job, before you guys started dating. I was busy with work and a shitty friend. It wasn't until about a month before you guys broke up, when I moved back, that we became close again. I was her person when you disappeared."

"Why didn't it work out with you two?"

Carefully considering my response, I reply, "We had an amazing time. But honestly? I was afraid of her. Women like Emma are… Well, they're the ones you settle down and have kids with. I wasn't ready for that, and neither was she. So, we made the mutual decision to just be friends. We couldn't imagine a life without each other in it. She's my best friend and has been for the last two decades. I never had a desire to date her after that, because I knew that if I did and it didn't work out, I'd lose her."

"You're okay with being friend-zoned forever?" His expression says it all—he needs to know that I'm not a threat.

I huff a laugh. "I mean, wouldn't you? If you had the choice of being her best friend, or never seeing her again, wouldn't you do the same thing?" He nods in agreement, so against my better judgment, I continue, "But you aren't going to be her best friend, I already hold that title. However, I have a better idea."

I can't believe I'm about to say this…

"So, here's the thing. She called an emergency buffalo plaid meeting tonight with the girls. Before you ask, it's something Lily, Riley, and Emma started for when they had a bad day or needed girl time. They get together to wear hideous pajamas, eat a bunch of junk food, drink too much wine, and watch horribly predictable romance movies. You know, the ones where some dude saves a hot chocolate stand or Christmas tree farm in the name of love."

"Why are you telling me this?"

Do I need to spell it out for him? Fuck, he's dense.

"Because if she needs a buffalo plaid night, it means you're important enough to her that she asked for it in the first place. She wouldn't need her girlfriends if I hadn't tried to piss you off." I pause for a moment as our waitress drops off our order, then continue, "I want to do right by her. If you two are supposed to ride off into the sunset together like some kind of *Pride and Prejudice* reboot, I need to know what your intentions are."

He takes a bite of his burger. Once he's done chewing, he replies, "Why do I think this would be more of an interrogation than her dad?"

"Because it is. Her dad, Joe, would murder you. Don't worry, I'll help him hide the body." I shrug. "Answer the question."

"I want to marry her. Not today, not tomorrow, but one day. Well, that's actually a lie. If she told me today that she wanted to run off to City Hall, I would marry her without a second thought. She isn't there yet, and it doesn't help that we are technically on a break right now."

I interrupt, "A break? Shit, man, I'm sorry. I didn't know she took it that far. But, so help me, if you hurt her again by cheating because you were *on a break...*"

"I would never. I plan on spending the rest of my life showing her how much I love her. If that means giving her space right now, I'll do it. I just want to make sure she knows just how extraordinary she is. She's the love of my life—there's no one else, there will never be anyone else.

After what you told me, though, I just hope I am good enough for her."

"You're not, but damn, that's a good answer."

Dylan chuckles, and after taking a drink of his water, he continues, "The reason I disappeared on her all those years ago was the same reason you two decided to stay friends— she scared me too. I knew it in my bones that she was it for me, but I'm man enough now to admit that leaving her was the biggest mistake of my life. I need to win her back."

I want Emma to be happy, even if it's with this pointless white crayon. If he hurts her again, I'll gladly rearrange his face like a shitty feng shui tutorial video.

My brilliant idea will not only put me in Emma's good graces but might salvage her relationship with Dylan. I pull out my phone to text Lily. "Hold on a sec, I need to message someone." He nods and continues eating his lunch.

I don't see what the appeal is. Sure he's hot, but that's about it. But if Emma wants me to play nice with the grouch, I'll play nice.

> Okay if I bring a plus 3?

LILY

> Guys or girls? I don't think Emma needs a why choose romance right now.

> No, it's for you sweetheart! Time to spice things up with Andrew!

> I mean... 🥴

> I'm kidding!

> But in all seriousness, I finished a hot regency romance novel that's like if Jane Austen decided to join a poly knot, if you want to borrow it.

> That's not why I'm texting you. Please don't hate me, I want to invite Dylan and his girls.

What are you up to?

Amazing surprise for Emma!

> I get to be the hero. And she gets to live happily ever after with Mr. Darcy. If I don't kill him first.

Aww, you called him Mr. Darcy!

> That is not a compliment. If I wanted to compliment him, I would have called him Colonel Brandon or Edward Ferrars. Now they had game!

I am not going to ask how you know that, but I'm here for it!

I won't tell Em, but do you think this is a good idea?

It's my idea, so obviously it is.

I hope you're right!

Even I'll admit this is probably the stupidest idea I've ever come up with, but I love Emma and want her to have a happily ever after.

Ugh, why does it have to be with an unwicked candle of a man?

I sigh and open my web browser on my phone to send Lily a copy of Emily Rath's books that I mentioned to her, with overnight delivery—who doesn't love a book where three hot men want you and each other? It's time for Lily to take a break from cartoon cover romcoms and dial up the spice!

With that settled, I need to order hideous plaid pants for this little intervention. "All right, send me your address, I'll be there around 5:30, I have to do a pick-up order first. What size pants do you and your girls wear?"

He stops with his burger an inch from his mouth and sets it down. "Why the fuck are you asking about my daughters' pants?"

"Sorry, did you not hear I'm putting in an order? Oh, shit, sorry. I just realized I had that whole conversation without you. Here's the synopsis for you: You love Emma; I love Emma; I want Emma to be happy; even if it's with you. So, I'm going to save the day."

"I'm not following…"

"Of course you're not. Keep up, Ben Affleck knockoff. I'm picking you up tonight; you're coming to Lily's; you're bringing your girls; you're joining in for buffalo plaid night. In the end, I'm going to be the Man of Honor at the wedding, and plan the damn thing at cost. You'll mention in your speech that I'm the hero in your story… And I'll go home with a bridesmaid, or groomsman. The end."

Damn, I'm good!

"We're on a break. I don't think she wants to see me after yesterday."

"Yes, she does. Emma's my best friend; I know her better than you. If we do this, you need to show her that you're just there to spend time with her… *not naked*. Hence, the kid buffer. I know you guys can't keep your hands off each other when you're in the same room for ten seconds."

"Why are you doing this?"

I get it, he doesn't trust me. I wouldn't trust me either if I was in his bargain-bin loafers. "I told you, I was an asshole yesterday and need to make it up to Emma."

"Let me check with the girls and see if they want to come. If they are, I'm in."

"Great, it's settled. Lunch is on you, right? Since I am kind of saving the day and all." Keith never charges me, but I'm not about to let Dylan know that.

He laughs. "Sure."

We finish lunch and go our separate ways. After receiving a text from him with sizes for the three of them, place an online order, and pick it up on my way home.

Time to save the day!

Ethan is right on time, pulling up to my house at exactly 5:30. The girls and I talked today about how I'm dating Emma—which they already figured out when they met her at the bookstore. They were entirely too excited about it. After being honest with them about what happened with Emma, both are on-board with Ethan's plan and agreed to come along.

I invite him in and he hands me a bag with black and white pajama pants for the three of us; he's already wearing his. We get changed and leave a few minutes later. The girls are giggling to each other about tonight and it actually helps to ease my nerves that they want to be part of this with me.

On the way to Lily's, Ethan asks the girls about school and books they are reading. They debate who the biggest villain is in the book Lizzy's reading. I can see why Emma likes Ethan so much, he gets along with everyone.

We pull up to the house and I'm nervous all over again. *What if this doesn't work?* "Are you sure this is a good idea?"

"Nope. This could go south the moment we walk in the door. Or... it will be amazing and you'll thank me on the drive home for my absolute brilliance. I plan large scale events and weddings for a living, I think I can plan crashing a pajama party with precision."

I hope he's right.

As we make our way up the driveway, he pats me on the shoulder. "I got this, Mayo."

Mayo?

He leads the way, opening the front door without knocking. "The party has arrived!" We follow him into the house, closing the door behind us. Ethan hands Lily a pair of pajama pants and she laughs hysterically; must be an inside joke.

Lily spots us behind Ethan. "Oh my gosh! Hi girls! I haven't seen you since, what, Christmas?" She glances behind her. "Andrew is somewhere around here, and... Riley, come over here for a second, I want to introduce you to Harriet and Lizzy!" Riley joins Lily and greets the girls. "Hey, all of the kids are upstairs playing video games and reading. The girls are welcome to head up if they like. The movie we're going to watch isn't exactly five-star. Can I get anyone something to drink?"

Riley rolls her eyes. "Lily, for the love, please let them come inside and get settled?"

In the corner of my eye, I spot Ethan talking to Emma. She doesn't appear too happy to see me. "Uh, a beer would be great, if you have one?" I ask weakly. This was all a big mistake and I'm going to lose Emma.

Lily follows my line of sight—obviously I'm not being covert enough. Leaning in with a quiet voice, she assures me, "It's okay, she's just surprised. Come on, go have a seat and I'll grab you one. Stout or IPA?"

"IPA would be great, thanks." Lily is so welcoming, but I hope she's right and this whole thing doesn't blow up in my face.

I glance over to Ethan again. He leans in to kiss Emma on the cheek before gesturing toward me. Last night, I would've wanted to punch a wall if I saw it. After getting to know him a little, he isn't a threat where Emma is concerned, and I find myself grateful that she has someone in her corner that's protective of her.

Emma hesitantly walks up to me, and I'm suddenly over-come with worry that she might ask me to leave. "Hey, I didn't know you were coming."

"Sorry, Ethan invited me, but I can go if you want?" *Please don't ask me to.*

"No, no, stay. Ethan told me you two talked." Her gaze falls to the floor, fidgeting with the hem of her shirt.

I reach out my hand and take hers. "Hey, I don't want you to feel uncomfortable. I didn't mean to crash your girls' night."

She notices our matching pants, and lets out a soft laugh. Her eyes lift to meet mine with a small smile. "Nice pants."

I lean in next to her ear and whisper, "At least I'm wearing pants, unlike some people I know who answer the door half naked." Emma stifles a laugh; she's trying to keep it together. So am I. When I pull back, I lose myself in her eyes for a moment.

"I hope you don't mind cheesy, predictable romance movies."

"Can't say I've ever seen one, but I'll watch whatever you want. I just wanted to spend time with you, if that's okay?" My response earns me another smile, but she lets go of my hand, stuffing both of hers in her pockets. I clear my throat. "Lily told me to go sit, and you know how she can be when we don't follow her marching orders. Want to join me?"

"Sure." Her eyes find mine every few steps as we walk over to the living room.; she's struggling to wrap her head around all this. We sit together and I have the urge to place my hand on her thigh, but instead place my arm on the back of the couch behind her. She sits so stiffly, definitely as nervous as I am, and thankfully she breaks our now almost awkward silence. "I didn't see the girls before they headed upstairs. How are they doing?"

I lean in a few inches, so only she can hear me. "They were excited to come and nerd out with Lily's kids and your boys."

Emma looks down at my lips, then back up. If this was yesterday, I would close the distance and kiss her. It feels almost as if she's going to go for it, but instead sucks in a breath and turns away to stare ahead. Her cheeks are a bright crimson and it reminds me of when we first met all over again. I don't look away, instead bringing my other hand to her chin to gently turn her face to look at me. I'm about to tell her how much it means to me that she is okay with my being here, but we're interrupted by Lily.

"Hi, hey, um… Here's your IPA. Em, I got you a glass of Sauv Blanc. Sorry, I don't keep gin in the house. Or limes. Or tonic. I don't know how you two can stand the stuff. Tastes like a forest." She hands us our drinks and scurries off.

"Thanks, Lil!" Emma calls after her.

"So, what is this whole pajama party about?" I know the answer, but I want her to talk to me.

She clears her throat. "Oh, it's silly really. It all started a few years ago when Riley had a bad day at work. I went to the store and bought fuzzy socks, matching pajama pants, the makings for a killer charcuterie board, and a crap ton of wine. We put on a Christmas movie where the small town guy owns a bookstore, or a hardware store, or coffee shop… I don't remember. I think the woman came from some big city to buy it out, or whatever. They fell in love and saved Christmas." She takes a sip of her wine. "Now, every time we have a rough day or we're celebrating, we recreate it."

Ethan walks over, pulling our attention to him. "So, can I count bringing him as an early Christmas present? Or does this have me covered until your birthday? I mean, you guys kissed and made up, right? I know, I know, you don't have to thank me. You're welcome." He winks and walks away without waiting for Emma's answer.

"I'm sorry about him. I know he's a lot." She takes a big gulp of her wine, looking especially cute when she's anxious like this.

I move my lips right next to her ear and it causes her to shiver. I know I shouldn't rile her up, but I can't help it. If I can't touch her, I want her to feel me everywhere. "I'm not sorry, E. You were right; he's actually a good guy. If it wasn't for him, I wouldn't be here with you tonight."

As I pull back, I press a soft kiss on her cheek. She hums in approval and there are little goosebumps along her arms. I love that after all this time, I can have that effect on her. Especially after everything.

Riley joins us on the couch next to Emma. "Okay, love birds, we are putting on the movie in a minute." She addresses me directly, pointing her finger. "You better not say a word. We know it's not Oscar worthy, but if you say *anything* about *anything* regarding this movie, I will personally remove you from this house."

"Yes, ma'am." I don't know Riley, but she has a confidence about her that when she speaks, you listen.

I call out for the girls to see if they want to join us, but they insist that they would rather hang out upstairs playing video games. Moving my arm from the couch, I switch my beer from one hand to the other to keep myself from touching her. After last weekend, all I want to do is have her hand in mine. Ethan's right—I can't keep my hands to myself when it comes to her.

We remain close to watch the movie, though only our shoulders and thighs are touching. About three minutes in, I feel her pinky tap mine. I look at her from the corner of my eye and wrap my pinky around hers. She brushes a soft kiss to my cheek, then rests her head on my shoulder.

"I'm sorry, Emma." I keep my voice low. She nods in response before going back to watching her movie.

The next hour is a blur. I hardly pay attention to the movie; I'm too busy stealing glances every chance I get. Emma surprises me when she moves her hand, letting go of my pinky to interlace our fingers, and lets out a sigh. A minute or two later, I feel it—three squeezes. I pause for a second. *Did I imagine it?* Once my heart restarts, I squeeze back three times.

"Hey, can we talk later?" She doesn't look at me when she says it, but I don't care.

"Of course." I kiss the top of her head as she rests on my shoulder again.

Whatever this woman wants, I'll give her.

She loves me.

24

EMMA

From the moment I met Dylan, we've always had incredible chemistry. Even now, years later, when I see him, my breath hitches and the butterflies in my stomach start doing parkour. There's no point in fighting it. I tried and failed. Sure, he's easily the most attractive man I have ever known, but it's more about how he only sees me. He strips me bare, seeing my good with my bad, and wanting all of it. There's always so much fire and passion coming from him, and it's all focused on me.

I've never met another man who makes me feel this way, so when Ethan brought him to Lily's, my emotions were all over the place. I wanted some space, but also wanted him to take me in his arms and never let go. The moment he walked in, wearing matching pajama pants with his girls, I was a goner. Ethan rushed over to apologize, telling me that it was his idea after he had lunch with Dylan. If my overprotective best friend can come around to the idea of Dylan and I dating again, why shouldn't I?

After the movie, Ethan rounded up all the kids and met us at the front door. It was a school night, so Dylan and his kids needed to get home, and mine needed to get to bed. He helped get all the kids in our cars, giving me a few moments with Dylan.

When Dylan kissed me—*okay, I kissed him first*—it was so full of the love and the promises we haven't spoken. I'll never forget how he whispered in my ear, "I want to be the last man who kisses you," before he got in Ethan's car to go home.

Once the kids were in bed, he called me, but only to set up a time for coffee. He told me he wanted to make time for us to properly date and that he wanted to be sure to respect my boundaries. Most of our time together has been very intimate, and we need more baseball games, dinners, or even just lunch in the middle of a work day. Basically, we need to stay in public.

As I walk up to the very same coffee shop that we ran into each other a few weeks ago, I take a deep breath before opening the door. Dylan beat me here, *because of course he did*. I was hoping for a few moments to collect myself. I'm barely a foot in the door when he's out of his seat and headed my way. He's wearing dark gray slacks, a black button-down collared shirt, and… his glasses. I'm such a sucker for those damn black-framed glasses of his. He typically has contacts, and rarely wears them. It's like catnip for me when he does.

He wraps me in a friendly hug and kisses my temple. "You came."

"That's what she said," I mutter, the words slipping out before I can stop them. He heard me and thankfully laughs.

As he releases me, he takes my hand and leads me to the cashier. "Usual?"

"I don't think they serve gin and tonics here, Dylan." I quirk an eyebrow at him.

He bites his lip, and replies with a smile, "Of course not. I meant a Thai coconut milk tea with large pearl boba." I shouldn't be surprised that he remembers; he always does. I nod and he orders for both of us. Once they're ready, we sit at the table I originally found him at.

"So…" I don't know what to say. I wish I did, but I just don't.

Dylan dives right in. "E, I'm sorry for everything. I'm sorry for hurting you all those years ago. I'm sorry for taking things too fast. I'm sorry for losing my shit on Ethan. But mostly, I'm sorry I didn't trust you." It comes out in rapid succession and I'm stunned into silence as he continues, "I will never hide how I feel about you. I made the mistake of trying to pick up where we left off, even though you didn't want to, and I blew it. It's just… When you're not with me, it's like something's missing—something I didn't know I needed in my life, until I got a little message on my phone that said '*hey*.'"

I smile and chuckle softly, remembering that night. I still can't believe my impulsive friends.

"I know it was Lily, or Riley, or both of them. I hoped that, even though they sent it, maybe there was the slightest chance I could win you back. But then I threw it all away by not trusting you." He looks down at his coffee, then back at me through his lashes. "Can we start over?"

I think of all of the famous movie and book quotes. Nothing does it justice. Instead, I speak from the heart. "Yes."

It's not the most profound thing to say in the world, but how can I follow all of that? He still loves me. If we're truly starting over, we might be able to move past my hurt. We both know where this is headed. It's only a matter of time.

"If you're okay talking about it, I want to know more about what happened the other night. I've met Aiden a few times now, and he's such a cool kid. I've only parented neurotypical kids, so I want to know more about raising a kid with sensory differences. What causes a meltdown for him? Does he have any special interests?"

Someone did their homework.

"Where do I start? It's a spectrum, so it's different for everyone. For Aiden, he struggles with textures, specifically clothes. He also doesn't always pick up on social cues, so he'll interrupt me when I'm talking to someone, or doesn't know what volume his voice should be in certain settings. He is so freakin' smart, and has a photographic memory. If you show him something, he'll remember it forever. He's obsessed with fantasy books, and wants to be a wizard when he grows up. Fair warning, Ethan and Aiden bond over that. It's kind of their thing. But, Aiden loves sharing with anyone who will listen. But honestly, other than that, I can't tell you much because I'm not autistic myself. All I can share is what it's like to be a parent of someone who thinks and feels differently. For me, that means I always have to be a step ahead to make sure he stays safe."

He listens intently as I continue, "That night there was a change in barometric pressure with the storm coming in, and it hurt his head enough that he couldn't articulate what he was feeling. My sitter couldn't figure out what was wrong, and luckily some time in a sensory swing helped him before I got home. It's why I was so short with you. When he's having a sensory meltdown, my priority is to make sure he is safe and help him self-regulate. It's like a flight, fight, or freeze response. Two nights ago, he was in flight mode, meaning that he wanted to escape his room, the house, and needed to be anywhere except where he was. We've taught him a lot of ways to help with the anxiety, but sometimes he just needs mom to help him calm down."

"That makes a lot of sense. My sister has anxiety. She freezes when an attack comes on. Not to compare it to what an autistic person experiences, I'm sure it's totally different, but I know it can be hard to watch someone you love when they are in the middle of it. I usually felt helpless, when we were younger. Is Aiden doing okay now, since the storm passed?"

"Yes, I'm sorry for not explaining all of this to you before. We are just usually, um…"

"I know," he sighs. I bite my bottom lip, trying my best not to think about it. "That's my fault. I struggle to keep my hands to myself with you."

I avert my gaze and shake my head. "It isn't just you."

Thankfully, he changes the subject, and we continue talking about our kids. His oldest, Harriet, is having boy problems and he doesn't know how to deal with any of it. I'm sure, if given the opportunity, he would ban her from dating until she turns thirty. She's decided she wants to be an author, and even though it's years from now, she's looking into colleges that have strong creative writing departments. Lizzy always has her nose stuck in a book, which is probably why Aiden clung to her when they met.

I tell him a bit about my step-sister, Charlotte. She has ADHD and received a very late diagnosis of autism; girls always fly under the radar. It wasn't until she was an adult, after Aiden was diagnosed, that she looked into it for herself. She calls herself 'neurospicy' and I love that she embraces it. Char has helped me understand Aiden so much more than any book I've read. We talk at least once a week, but she lives across the country in New York and it can be rough. I miss her so much.

After about an hour, we head to the bookstore, hand in hand, so I can pick up a few books for my boys. A few steps before we reach the door, he stops us in our tracks, surprising me as he pulls me to him, wrapping me in his arms.

"Before we go in, E, I only have one question for you. Are you available to grab a drink or dinner to… discuss a few things?" His beautiful dimples are on full display.

I can't help but laugh at the callback to our past. "Yeah, I'll have dinner with you. As long as it's not a business thing."

After the last three weeks of actual dates—in public, where neither of us end up naked—I feel like we've gotten to know each other again. We have a long way to go, but we're on the right track. It has taken restraint on both our parts to not strip each other down and take things too far, but it seems to be working. Maybe this time, we'll get it right.

I've fallen in love with him. There's no point in running from it anymore. I love his drive and ambition, and how he supports me in my goals and dreams. I'm up for President in the next few months, and he's excited that I'm doing big things. He claims I'm his missing piece, but really, he's mine.

Dylan's work party is tonight and he invited me to come as his plus one. Jason was able to take the boys a day early so I could attend. I'm eternally grateful that he's such a great dad, and after all these years, an amazing friend. I told him about how I was seeing Dylan again, and not that I was looking for his blessing, he encouraged me to see where it goes.

I'm still getting ready downstairs when there's a knock at the door. "It's open!"

The front door opens and closes. "Oh, love, you look *ravishing!*"

"Ethan! What are you doing here? Dylan will be here any minute and I'm not ready!"

He dusts invisible lint from his suit jacket. "Well, darling, Dylan asked me to pick you up—something about running late and not trusting rideshares. Anyway, I'm dropping you off at his party. I have an event ten minutes from there first thing in the morning, so I was going to be in the area anyway. Didn't he text you?"

I check my phone. "Shoot, it was on silent!"

DYLAN

Hey, gorgeous. Last minute change of
plans. I'll need to meet you at the party. I
texted Ethan and he said he can take you.
Hope that's okay?

I look back to Ethan. "Sorry, I didn't see it 'til now. I'll be ready in five."

Ethan looks me up and down, then raises an eyebrow. "In that? You look like you're about to attend a funeral. Come on, march your sexy ass upstairs; we're going to find you something that is just one level above naked. You need to get laid tonight, and there's no way it's going to happen in whatever the hell you want to call *this*." He gestures to my dress and I laugh as he drags me by the wrist up the stairs. We sift through my closet and he takes out a deep v-neck black dress and forces it into my hands. "This one. I'll be downstairs."

I get changed and the dress is sexy enough to turn heads, while still being work appropriate. I'm positive Dylan will not be able to keep his hands to himself tonight and I smile at the thought. As I head downstairs, I feel like I'm part of a grand reveal in a romcom movie.

Ethan confirms with his usual sexy grin. "*Yes!* You look incredible, Em! Are you sure this Dylan guy is the one? Because if not, I'll gladly take his place."

"Oh come on. You would throw away your single life of hot guys and girls in your bed every night?" I can't keep a straight face as we both crack up.

Ethan will probably be a perpetual bachelor. If he ever settles down, they will be one lucky person. He dated Chris for a while. Unfortunately, he did a number on Ethan—

even if he won't admit it. Three days after their break up, Ethan had a gorgeous woman on his arm at some gala in Paris, but he was still hung up on his ex.

We drive to the party, singing along to our favorite nineties and two-thousands pop the whole way. I'm genuinely happy; it's been a while since I've felt this way. I have amazing friends, my kids are awesome, I am up for promotion at work, and have a smokin' hot boyfriend. For the first time in a long time, everything feels in sync.

As we pull up to the swanky hotel, Ethan takes my hand, sensing I'm a little nervous. "You know, love, I was kidding about the getting laid part. Sure, you deserve all the orgasms in the world, but don't sleep with him if you feel you have to because of some arbitrary timeline that society dictates. If you want to, go for it, but he'll be fine either way. His dick won't fall off."

Ethan always knows exactly what to say. "Thank you. Well, don't wait up!" I give him a quick peck on the cheek before I exit the car and close the door behind me.

He rolls down the window to reply, "Oh, don't worry about me, I have my own date tonight. Have fun!"

I walk inside and pull out my phone to let Dylan know Ethan dropped me off. As I type out the message, I feel the air change around me before two arms wrap me from behind. The scruff of his five o'clock shadow tickles me as he softly kisses my neck.

"You look good enough to eat." His voice is low and sultry. The dress is already doing its job.

Tucking my phone back in my purse, I turn in his arms and wrap mine behind his neck. He wore his glasses tonight, and damn, *he* looks good enough to eat. With the way he's looking at me, with so much hunger in his eyes, I'm already turned on from his gaze alone.

Maybe the dress was a bad idea.

"You don't look half bad, yourself, Mr. Alexander." I pull him to me until our lips meet, and a growl rumbles in his chest as he kisses me. I'm in trouble. He's one step away from finding a dark corner, so I quickly step away. "Come on, we need to get to your party."

"Fuck the party." Dylan's completely serious. "I would rather spend the evening just you and me." He corrects himself, "Not for that. Well, I don't know if I'll be able to keep my hands off you in that dress, but let's go have a night on the town instead."

"You need to make an appearance. Come on, it could be fun! Like the old days." I shimmy out of his hold, which earns me one of his boyish grins as lets me go.

He takes my hand, and I squeeze it three times. Bringing our interlocked hands to his lips, he grumbles, "Fine, but we'll leave whenever *I* want."

"Deal." While I haven't told him I love him—not with words, at least—I honestly do. It's bigger than that, I have fallen *in love* with him again. I haven't felt this way about a man, since, well, him. This time it's different. He's different.

We walk inside where there are dozens of round tables draped in white linens, set for dinner. He leans in and whispers, "Would you mind grabbing us a couple of drinks? I need to say hi to a guy over there and I want an out for the conversation. When you come up, please tell me that you need to speak to me about something, *anything*." We used to play this game at events when we were younger. I smile at him and nod before wandering over to the bar.

The bartender addresses me and I order two gin and tonics, mine with extra lime. The night feels nostalgic, so why not keep it going? I take our drinks and make my way over to him.

There are four men standing with him, and a woman to his right who is laughing entirely too hard at something he said—obviously flirting with him. I don't feel any pang of jealousy. I feel… nothing. *Huh, that's weird.* It isn't, though, I know how much he cares about me, and I'm not worried about a beautiful woman shamelessly flirting with my man. I'm the one who gets to go home with him.

Dylan has a huge smile that reaches his eyes when he spots me approaching. *See, he's mine.* I hand him his drink, and with his free hand he guides me by the small of my back to join their conversation. "Everyone, this is Emma. Emma, this is Bryan, Tony, Rodger, and… Sorry, I don't remember your name?"

She lets out something that's a cross between a scoff and a laugh. "Isabelle. Hello, Emma." My name on her tongue is laced with resentment—she does *not* like me.

Dylan ignores her and continues talking to the men. "Emma is VP at a literary agency; she's absolutely brilliant."

"Literary agency?" Rodger asks. "Like book publishing?"

"Yes, we offer full-service for authors including representation, editing, and marketing."

Dylan adds, "She's up for promotion, actually. About to take over the book world."

Roger's eyes light up. "My wife reads a ton and likes to review the books she finishes on social media."

I excitedly whip out my phone. "Really? Can I have her handle? I always love meeting other people who love reading as much as I do."

He smiles and pulls out his phone to find the information, and it looks like we love reading all of the same books—even the spicy ones.

Dylan clears his throat. "So…"

Oh, right, I was supposed to get him out of this.

"Sorry everyone, I forgot I promised someone I would introduce them to Dylan. I'll bring him right back, I promise!" He smiles at me, so much mischief in his eyes. We shake everyone's hands and walk away.

"I'm sorry about that Isabelle woman. I promise I wasn't flirting with her."

I frown at him. "Why are you sorry? I trust you, and I don't think you would be dumb enough to hit on another woman while you have this as a date." I gesture to my dress and beam at him.

Dylan's eyes slowly rake down my body, showing off his gorgeous dimples while he bites his lower lip. His gaze makes me a little self conscious—I feel naked. Bringing his drink to his lips, he says into his glass, "You are a hell of a lot more than just my date, Emma."

Someone walks up to talk to us before I can ask what he

meant, but he never takes his eyes off me as they ask, "Hey, Dylan, how's it going?"

Dylan reluctantly turns to address him, "Hey, good to see you, Matt."

Matt is about to ask Dylan something, but then does a double take, looking at me curiously. "I'm sorry, have we met? You look so familiar."

"Oh, I don't think so. I haven't been to one of these in years." He looks familiar too, but I can't place him.

Dylan wraps his arm around me, placing his hand on my hip. His thumb strokes back and forth, sending fireworks through me. "You might remember her from a *long* time ago. Emma and I used to attend events and mixers back in the day." I can barely focus on what he's saying; my body is on fire.

Matt's eyes widen. "*See*, I knew I recognized you! You were Dylan's girlfriend."

"No longer past tense," Dylan replies matter-of-factly, with a hint of a growl.

And there's the possessive Dylan I haven't seen in a while.

I make light of it. "Plot twist! But you know, now that I think about it, I remember you. You were one of my friend's clients when I worked for the magazine. Wow, you haven't changed a bit." Dylan squeezes my side.

Easy there, tiger, I'm not flirting. I'm yours.

Matt laughs. "Katie? Man, that takes me back. That was, what? Fifteen years ago?" He shakes his head. "So, you guys are dating again? That's wild! Guess you should have wifed her up the first time." I stiffen a little at those words. Back then, that's exactly where I thought we were headed.

"Oh, I plan on doing it this time around." Dylan mutters it under his breath to himself, but I still hear him. I have a feeling Matt did too, based on his smirk. The thought has crossed my mind, but we haven't really talked about it, we're trying to take things slow.

"Well, it's great to see you again. What are you up to these days?" Matt asks me.

I tell him briefly how I got into publishing. Matt tells me about how he and Dylan are going to be working together again soon. After several minutes, I feel a slight pinch on my hip—he wants an out again.

"Well, Matt, I'm sorry to do this, but I need a refill on my drink. It was great catching up." We excuse ourselves and make our way to the bar for another round. Dylan wasn't kidding earlier, he hasn't stopped touching me since I arrived here.

We meet other people Dylan works with, and after what feels like the four-hundredth person he's introduced me to, my social battery is drained. I am not an extrovert. I'm able to pass as one in these settings, but it takes a toll on my energy. Dylan is the same way; we would both rather curl up on the couch with a good book than go out to these sorts of large events.

He leans in, his voice low enough that only I can hear, "I feel like you're itching to grab your ereader that I *know* is in your purse."

I had just taken a sip of my drink and almost spit it out laughing. "Can I?" I bite my lip and he's smiling ear to ear.

He adjusts his glasses. "Want to get out of here?"

"Yes, please!" I may have said it just a tad too loud and enthusiastically. He gently grips my chin and brings my lips to his. Dylan's kisses have been warm and sweet all night; he's holding back. "Did you get a room here, or do we have to head back home?"

"I got a two-room suite, just in case we had too much to drink."

Two rooms? Nope, cancel that reservation. We only need one, mister. And I'm going to ride you until my legs give out.

He laughs, and I realize there is a ninety-eight percent chance that I said that out loud. *Shit.* He takes my hand, and gestures to the exit. "E, I'm not canceling the reservation. I would like nothing more than to make love to you all night, but tonight, you're going to spend a few hours in my arms, decompressing from all this, then I'll stay in my own room. Last time I rushed this, I almost lost you. I'm not making that mistake again." Him not wanting to sleep with me just makes me want to sleep with him even more. "Come on, let's take a walk."

I am positive that my face is showing all of my emotions. While I am a little disappointed that he doesn't want me tonight, I'm also thankful that he's been patient with me. Except, I don't want him to be patient anymore. I want to see him lose control; I'm ready for it.

We walk along the marina, the moon's reflection following us. It reminds me of the cabin on the lake, so peaceful and quiet. Tonight's a little chilly and he offers me his jacket. I decline, but he doesn't listen, and drapes it over my shoulders anyway. I put it on all the way, wrapping myself in its warmth.

After a few minutes, panic surges inside me. I stop us in our tracks, which forces him to look at me. "Everything okay?"

"No, it's not actually. I just realized I forgot my bag in Ethan's car!"

He smiles and tugs at my hand to keep walking. "It's fine, I'll order something to be delivered to the hotel."

"That's a thing? I've done grocery delivery, but you can order clothes for same-day delivery too? This late at night?" I take out my phone. "What's the app? I'll order right now." He snatches my phone out of my grip, and throws it into the marina. I shriek, "What the hell, Dylan?"

A frown I haven't seen since I tried to order drinks at the baseball game appears. "You think I was going to let you pay for it?"

"Fine… but *my phone?*" I gesture to the water, where the fishes are no doubt scrolling my social media feed.

"I'll buy you a new one that'll be here in the morning. In the meantime, call Ethan from my phone, explain that I tossed yours into the water when you tried to pay for something, and that Jason can call me if the kids need to reach you. He'll get it."

Dylan hands me his phone. This whole thing is so strange, but I do what he asked and call Ethan, who laughs hysterically at Dylan's tossing my phone into the water. He agrees to call Jason to let him know about my phone situation. I hang up and hand his phone back to Dylan.

"See, it's settled." He pockets his phone. "Now, let's get back to the hotel, order some food because that dinner was horrible and I know you only ate two bites. I'll make sure you have new clothes, too."

"Dylan, this is… I don't know what this is. I know you have to be doing okay financially, but *so am I*. I don't need you to pay for anything." It's awkward discussing this with him.

"I know, but I have more money than I know what to do with, and I want the chance to dote on you. I like taking care of you, and it means more to me because I know you can take care of yourself."

The words slip out. "I love you." My hands cover my mouth, my eyes wide as soon as I say them. "Sorry, that was *not* the best time to say that. It's just… nope." I hold my ground, straightening my posture. "I'm retracting that apology, and I won't take back what I said, because it's true." My arms stretched wide, I confess again, "I'm in love with you, Dylan. I'm sorry it's coming out this way. I loved you all those years ago, but this is different." I retreat, pulling the jacket around me, feeling vulnerable. "You're different, we're different… and now I'm rambling. I'm going to stop talking n—"

He cuts me off by grabbing each side of my face, bringing his lips to mine in a tender but sizzling kiss I feel all the way to my toes.

"Say it again," he whispers into my mouth.

"I love you?"

Dylan smiles against my lips. "Again." He wraps his arms around me and holds me tight. I didn't realize how much these three little words meant to him, until now.

I let out a light laugh. "I love you, Dylan." As much as it pains me to do it, I stop his heated kisses to explain myself.

"I don't love you because of the material stuff, I hope you know that."

"How could you, E? You have no idea how much money I even have. I love that you don't need me to help with anything. You're going to take over the world, remember? I want to be there for all of it, but I also want to spoil you— especially since I know you hate it. You know I loved you when we were basically kids. But now? I love you as a man who plans on spending the rest of his life showing you how incredible you are." He tucks a few wind swept strands of hair behind my ear. "You are my everything, Emma. I'm so in love with you, I can't imagine my life without you in it." A shiver shoots down my arms from his words. "You're cold. Come on, let's get back."

"Just please don't throw any more of my belongings in the marina," I plead. With a quick kiss to my forehead, he releases me and we walk hand in hand back to the hotel.

25

DYLAN

She loves me. Not past tense. The woman I've loved for the majority of my adult life loves me. While I know with all of my being that she does, hearing the words from her lips is better than anything I ever could've imagined.

She. Loves. Me.

I haven't told Emma exactly how much money I have, I know it doesn't matter to her. If—*when*—we marry, she won't need to work another day in her life. I'd never want her to give up her dream job. If I ever suggested it, she'd throw my money into the marina to live with her phone. And I'd deserve it.

Keeping my promise, I didn't cancel the reservation for the two-room suite. It's the biggest one they have; I want to spoil her, and also want to keep her trust. Emma's mine, tonight isn't about sleeping together.

We make our way to the front desk to get the keys. Before the woman greets us, Emma catches me off guard, addresses her first. "Hi there, this gorgeous man has a reservation under Dylan Alexander." She turns to me. "It's under your name, right?" I nod, and she continues, "Great, well he reserved a two-room suite, and we are going to only need the one. Can we change the reservation?" I bite back my smile at how my woman takes charge. *My woman.* Fuck, it feels good to say that again.

"E, it's fine," I tell her quietly. I won't be able to keep my hands to myself unless we have the two rooms. Even then, it's going to be torture. I need to tread carefully; I'm not about to let her slip through my fingers again by moving too fast. Checking the name tag, I address the receptionist, "Jessica, that's not necessary, we'll keep it as is."

Emma's brows furrow. "Just for that, Mr. Alexander, you can have the couch."

Well, now she's just playing dirty.

Turning back to Jessica, Emma asks again, "Can we change it? I'll pay any difference." She knows damn well what will happen the moment she tries to pay. I'm tempted to grab her wallet from her purse and toss it in the water to live with her phone, just to prove a point.

"You win, beautiful." I shake my head with a chuckle, then pull out my card and hand it to her. "Change the room." She bites her lip with the most playful grin I've ever seen on her, and hands Jessica my card.

Once we have the keys, we take the elevator to our room on the top floor. About half way up, I resist the urge to hit the emergency stop button and rip that dress off of her right here.

This is going to be harder than I thought.

Emma's tucked into my side with my arm tightly around her. I'm afraid if I blink too long, she won't be here with me. I love having her so close and my hand *may* have traveled down to her ass. She doesn't protest or push away. Once we reach the top, I take her hand and guide her to the room.

"Here's your key."

She uses it to enter. The room is nothing short of spectacular, with an incredible view of the marina. "Oh. Are we in the right room? This looks like someone's house."

"Well, it's ours for the night." She turns to look at me, and I don't think I've ever set eyes on a more beautiful woman. "Before I forget, we need to get clothes ordered for you."

I pull up the app and hand my phone to her. After scrolling the options for a moment, she huffs a laugh. "I can't order these, they're incredibly expensive." She tries to hand my phone back to me, but I don't take it. "I'll just do my walk of shame when I leave here in this dress in the morning."

As I take a step toward her, my hand finds her hip as I slowly guide her backward. "And what would you be feeling ashamed about, beautiful?"

"I, uh…" She's flustered at first, but collects herself quickly, lifting her chin. "I, in fact, would have no shame." I slowly, one tortuous step at a time, continue to lead her to the wall behind her. I can't help myself, I want to push her up against it, tear that dress off, and brand every inch of her. Her breath hitches. "However, you're probably right. I don't think it would be ideal for you to be walking out of this hotel in the morning with me looking like a lady of the night. You are here for a work event, after all. So, fine, I'll buy pants and a shirt. But, I'm going to reimburse you for it."

"Good luck trying to pay me back without a phone," I tell her, and she playfully swats my chest before returning to her search for an outfit.

I lean in, propping myself up on the wall behind her as she clicks away. I wonder if she even notices, but her breathing picks up. *Oh, she noticed.* I keep my voice low. "I already ordered your phone. It should be delivered to the front desk first thing in the morning."

Emma's eyes narrow on me as she clicks the *buy now* button and hands my phone back. "Ordered. They should be here in a few hours. In the meantime, I am going to change into one of those fluffy robes I know they have from when I stayed here for a conference a year ago. Can you help me out of this dress?"

She guides me back a foot and turns. As I slowly unzip her dress, I can't help enjoying the feel of her soft skin as the zipper falls lower. *Fuck, she isn't wearing a bra or underwear.* I kiss her shoulder, her neck, and finally nip at her earlobe. Loving that she always smells like violets, I take a moment to breathe her in before growling, "Emma, where's your underwear?"

"What?" Holding her dress up over her breasts, she walks toward the bathroom to grab a robe. This devil of a woman knows exactly what she's doing, and it's working. She coyly glances over her shoulder. "Like I could wear a bra or panties with this dress." She continues to saunter off to the bathroom. My now incredibly hard cock is tenting my pants; not touching her tonight is going to be absolute torture.

Fuck. Why did I think this was a good idea?

Emma stops abruptly and drops her dress. It cascades down her body like a damn waterfall, leaving her bare, only wearing her heels. She steps out of it, turns on her heel, and prowls toward me. I shake my head, unable to hide my smile. *Wicked woman.*

"What are you doing, beautiful?"

Her response surprises me. "I'm taking what's mine."

This isn't the Emma I know, and I'm left speechless. Once she reaches me, she hooks her hand behind my neck and pulls my mouth to hers. We fight for the upper hand, tongues dueling, teeth clashing, there isn't anything gentle about this kiss. I bend to wrap her legs around my waist, needing her closer to me. She's claiming me as hers, but I am not about to let her. I want her to give herself to me, surrender our past, and let me take care of her.

"E, you know I'm yours, but are you sure about this?"

Between kisses, there is no hesitation as she replies, "I've never been so sure of anything in my life."

She's mine.

I slide her down my body until her feet hit the floor, then rip off my tie as she reaches for my belt buckle. I need to slow this down—I'm not about to come in my pants as she undresses me.

"No." I grab her wrist to stop her from taking off my slacks and kiss the inside of her wrist. "We aren't doing this."

Her chest rises and falls with heavy breaths, feeling everything I'm feeling. As it slows, she finally replies, sounding almost disappointed, "Oh, if you don't want to, that's okay."

Emma tries to look away, embarrassed by her actions. *Absolutely fucking not.* I gently grab the front of her throat to pull her mouth back to mine, wanting her to melt into me again.

Once she's no longer tense, I say into her mouth, "I don't think you get it." I kiss her cheek. "I…" I kiss her chin, my hand never leaving her neck that fits so perfectly in my hand. "Love…" My lips move to her jaw. "You." I kiss my favorite place on her neck, just below her ear. "I want to savor…" My mouth finds the one spot I know will drive her crazy, where her shoulder and neck meet. She moans the moment my lips touch it, making me smile into her neck. "Every moment." I pull back to look into her crystal blue eyes. "I've craved you for decades, please let me take my time."

With my hand claiming her like this, we both know there will be no savoring. I'm going to *devour* this woman. I bring her mouth back to mine and I can't stop kissing her. I'm addicted, unable to get enough. Emma's the last woman I want to kiss, the last woman I want in my bed. The moment she bites my bottom lip, I can't take it anymore. I want to own every part of her, make sure she knows she is mine, and not just for tonight. I pick her up again, loving the feeling of her legs wrapped around me, and walk into the bedroom.

I set her down on the bed and ask, "You were walking around all night with nothing under your dress?"

Smiling, she bites her lip that's still a little swollen from kissing me. "Well, I'll admit, I had to ditch the underwear in the bathroom earlier tonight. I swear I was wearing them. It's your fault, you wore your glasses." I unbutton and take off my shirt, making sure to keep my glasses on, just for her.

She reaches to take off her shoes, but I stop her, shaking my head with a look of warning. "Leave them on." I drop to my knees. I've been obsessing about the feeling of her coming on my tongue since the cabin. I grab behind her knees to bring her closer to me and kiss the inside of her thigh. "I don't know that I can be gentle with you."

Pausing, I wait for her response. Licking her lip, she finally replies, "I'm yours. I don't want you to be gentle. I want all of it."

I snap. Something primal inside me takes over the moment she tells me she's mine. I grab her legs, bringing them over my shoulders in one swift movement. "I expect at least three from you before I even push inside this sweet cunt." Sucking in a sharp breath, she lays her head back on the bed. "No, baby. I want to see your beautiful face as you give me every piece of you tonight." She boosts herself up on her elbows, giving me a beautiful view of her incredible tits. I start slow, teasing and pressing small kisses to the inside of her thighs. I pause when her head falls back. "Emma, what did I say? Eyes on me." She snaps up immediately, and I reward her with my mouth right where she wants it. "Good girl."

"Dylan," she cries out at first contact, and her head hangs back again.

"What did I say, baby?"

Emma's gaze snaps back to me, biting her lip. I take her with two fingers and massage the spot I know so well. I take my time building her up. "Right there, I'm close." Each time she tries to look away, I stop. She fights it, but eventually gives in. After all these years, I still instinctively know the perfect pressure and rhythm for her. I can feel her winding tighter and tighter. When she comes hard, she screams my name loud enough for anyone four floors below to hear.

Two to go.

"Attagirl. You're fucking stunning when you come undone for me. Two more, Emma. You give me two more, and I'll spend the rest of the night deep inside you, until you can't take it anymore." She's still coming down from her high but manages a nod. "If it's too much, or not enough, tell me." I'm so distracted by how amazing it is to have my face between her legs again that her sitting up startles me. "What is it, baby?"

"Condoms. They're in my bag that's still in Ethan's car." She chews on her lip, pausing for a moment. "I'm on the pill and, if you're okay with it, I'd rather have you inside me with nothing between us."

I haven't had unprotected sex in over a decade. The thought makes my cock twitch. Being inside her bare would be a dream. We used to go without when we were younger because she was always on the pill. I don't want anything between us, either. I trust Emma and honestly wouldn't even care if we used any kind of protection, because it's her. I've never thought about having more kids, but if she wanted to get pregnant, we would practice morning, noon, and night.

"Are you sure?"

"It wasn't just words, Dylan. I love you. I want to feel you come inside me. For me, this isn't just sex."

"It's never been just sex." I already miss the taste of her. I swirl my tongue around her clit, and she's a fucking dream, so wet for me as I push two fingers into her. Her walls clench, making my cock ache to be inside her. "Emma, you feel so amazing. I want nothing more than to have this tight pussy wrapped around my cock right now, but I still want two more from you first." I kiss the inside of her thigh. "Lay back, and let me take another." Her back arches as I murmur against her, "*Fuck*, I could spend the rest of my life with my face between your legs."

Emma laughs, but it's cut short when I add another finger. I love how she reacts to my touch and it only takes a minute to pull another orgasm from her.

Once she settles, she sighs. "Dylan, I don't have one more in me, it's too much."

I press one last kiss to her addicting pussy. "I know you can take it, you gave me three before, baby. But my only goal is to make you feel good right now. If you can only handle two, then two is enough for tonight. I meant what I said, you're mine now, just as I'm yours. We have all the time in the world to test your limits."

Before I crawl up on the bed with her, I take off her shoes and my clothes, leaving my boxer briefs on. Having her here with me, telling me she loves me, all I want is to take her right here. After the long night we've had, it can wait. She's mine, we can play another day.

Just as I'm about to settle in cuddled up behind her, she reaches her hand between us and grabs my cock. "Emma, this isn't about that." My voice is firm, but I don't stop her; it feels too damn good to have her touch me.

Shrugging out of my hold, she sits up. "I just needed a break." Her grip on me tightens. "I need you. Please."

Fuck, I can't say no to this woman. She could ask me for anything and I'd give it to her. I toss her onto her back and she chuckles. Moving off her for only a moment, I pull the belt from my pants on the floor, then grab both of her wrists. Pushing them above her head, I fasten the belt around them, wanting to control her pleasure. As I look down at her, giving herself to me like this, I nearly come all over her chest from the sight of her.

"Baby, you're so fucking beautiful. I don't think I'll last long with you all tied up for me like this." My lips find hers again as I take off my boxer briefs. I settle myself between her legs, my tip grazing her pussy. With my hand on the belt, keeping her arms above her head, and I groan into her mouth, "I hope you know that I intend to be the last man you'll ever be with. There's no coming back from this, beautiful."

I anticipate Emma pushing me back, maybe even ending this whole thing. Instead, she wraps her legs around me tighter, angling me so my cock slips into her hands-free. She's so wet that she takes me deep in one swift movement. The moan she lets out when I enter her will forever be burned into my brain.

Holding me there for a moment, she says softly, "I know."

Emma feels like heaven; the perfect fit. She always was. My mouth never leaves hers as I glide my free hand down her chest, past her stomach, and grip her ass to pull her to me as I push in as deep as she can take me. She lets out a cry, screaming my name. I begin moving in and out of her slowly, deliberately, wanting to be sure I hit right where she needs me. I need her to come for me one more time before I do. Managing to wriggle a hand free from the belt, she tangles her fingers into my hair and pulls me closer.

Sneaky woman.

My woman's taking what she wants and, as much as I love how she fights to gain control, I refuse to give in to her. I pull her hand from behind me, interlace our fingers, and hold it above her head again. With one hard thrust, I settle myself inside her, feeling her walls pulse around me.

"Tonight, you're *mine*, Emma."

Emma shakes her head. "Not just tonight."

"Then, be my good girl and give me all of you. Let go, baby."

As I continue rocking in and out of her, she kisses me with an intensity that I haven't felt before. The connection I have with her is consuming. I reach between us to massage her clit with my thumb, and it only takes one, two, three more thrusts before she bites down on my shoulder, her third orgasm shattering her.

"You're irresistible, a fucking goddess, Emma. I love it when you let go for me. You're going to give me one more. I want one more from you, baby." There's so much fire in her eyes. Not only is she not done, she needs more. "I know that look, E. What do you need?"

"Harder. I want it harder. I don't want to be able to walk for a week." Her voice is confident, commanding.

Oh, my sweet Emma, be careful what you wish for.

I release her hands above her head, and the belt is nowhere to be found. She pulls me closer, her nails digging into me.

I'm close, every thrust makes it harder to hold on for her to come with me. "*Fuck*, you take me so well, baby. But you don't need harder, you need me deeper." I pull away to flip her onto her stomach and lift her hips until my cock is lined up with her soaked pussy. I slide in with ease. "Make no mistake, your beautiful ass will be mine too, but not tonight. I need to prepare you for it."

Emma props herself onto her elbows and smirks over her shoulder. I pause for a moment, smirking back before I spank her ass. It isn't gentle, enough to make her clench around me and whimper in pleasure. I've dreamt about the sting on my palm as it hits, hearing the crack as it touches her. Nothing could have prepared me for the moans she releases. It turns her on as much as it does for me. She's clenching tighter around me, and I push in as far as she can take me.

Rubbing her now beautifully pink ass, I check in, "How are you feeling?"

"Again," she replies without flinching.

That's my girl.

I spank her two more times. Reaching to wrap her hair around my hand, I gently pull her toward me, forcing her back to my chest while still inside her. I release her hair and move my hand to the front of her throat, claiming one more part of her as mine.

Guiding her down onto me deeper, I tell her between thrusts, "You're perfect… like you were made for me, baby… I'm not going to stop…until you've come all over my cock, begging for more… Now give me what's mine. I want all of you, Emma."

She rests her head on me, giving me access to the side of her neck. I start at her shoulder, kissing up to where my fingers are still wrapped around her throat, and suck hard, branding her for the foreseeable future. *Mine.* I graze the now sensitive mark with my teeth, and she screams my name as she comes one more time.

"Good girl, just like that." I thrust in three more times before I come harder than I ever have in my life.

We sit there for a moment as I'm still nestled deep inside her. I wrap both my arms around her, kissing her shoulder. "*Fuck.* I have no words. You're fucking perfect."

Her hands fall to my embrace around her middle. "Mhm, I don't know if I can move." I nip at her ear, then slowly lift her off my cock; I'll be ready for another round if I stay inside her.

"I'll be right back, baby. Don't get up." I kiss her softly and slide off the bed and make my way to the bathroom. She has the cutest fucking grin that makes me want to jump right back into bed with her, but she needs time to recover.

In the bathroom, I quickly clean up and debate putting my boxer briefs back on. I want to sleep naked with her if she'll let me, but things are fragile right now. After deciding to put them on, I prepare a warm washcloth and a glass of water, and return to the bedroom. I hand her the water and gently clean up the mess we made between her legs, then make sure she finishes the whole glass—I need her hydrated for a possible round two. She did say she didn't want to walk for a week.

"Stay with me tonight? I was joking about the couch." Her voice is shaky, full of worry.

"Of course, beautiful, there's absolutely nowhere I would rather be. You think I'd leave the love of my life naked in bed like this? If I had it my way, we would never spend another night apart." She slides under the covers and I join her, stripping off my boxer briefs. I want every part of her pressed against me. After tonight, I don't know if I'll ever be able to spend a moment away from her.

Just as I think she's dozing off, she says into the dark, "I love you, Dylan."

My heart swells. "I love you too, beautiful... so much."

26

DYLAN

We had sex three times last night, and once this morning when she surprised me by joining me in the shower. *No, that wasn't sex, I made love to that incredible woman.* I'm addicted to her moans, how she tastes and feels, how her silky skin always smells like violets, and how blissfully happy she looks wrapped in my arms after she comes. It's more than how amazing she is in bed, I love her so fucking much and want to spend every day of the rest of my life with her. She's my other half. Dropping her off at home is going to hurt more than I'd care to admit.

While in the lobby retrieving her new phone and clothes, I'm waiting for the receptionist to grab everything, and open up my messages to text my sister.

> Are you free today around 2?

MELANIE
> Sure, what's up?

> I need to do some shopping and want your opinion.

Cryptic, but fine. Text me the address. I'll
be there.

I send her the address. Moments later, she responds.

Really?! Are you serious? Took you fucking
long enough.

I could really use Ethan's opinion on this, so I message him
as well.

Free around 2?

ETHAN

I'm not up for a threesome, maybe next
time?

You know damn well I'm not sharing Emma.

In fact, I plan on making that more
permanent.

No tattoos, either.

I reluctantly send him the address. He isn't going to have
the same response as Melanie, but he's Emma's best friend,
and I really need his help.

ETHAN

No. Absolutely not.

Guess I should just pick something online.

That should get his attention.

ETHAN

I thought you were kidding! You're actually
doing this?

I'll go, but only because I love Emma.

So help me, if you dare suggest anything less than perfection for her, I'm allowed to veto.

Seriously, we need to talk about this. I don't want her to freak out.

Thanks, I owe you one.

Yes, yes you do.

I pocket my phone and take the elevator back upstairs to Emma. Ethan's right, it has to be perfect.

We leave the hotel, and the drive home is filled with laughter, stories, and listening to an audiobook she put on. It's always so easy with her. My hand rests on her thigh for the entire drive, except for when my hand made its way into her pants. Or when she leaned over and took me in her mouth for the best blowjob of my life. It made trying to navigate through traffic incredibly difficult.

I drop her off at home, and as much as I want to come inside and claim her on every surface of her house, I have an appointment downtown.

I can't resist, pushing her up against the front entry to taste her one more time, making her come with her leg hooked over my shoulder and her hands in my hair. I'll be hard the rest of the day thinking about it, but worth being a few minutes late.

An hour or so later, I'm finally parked down the street from the store. Ethan beat me here and is waiting outside. "Hey, Ethan, thanks for coming." My smile hasn't left my face all day, but he doesn't return it.

"I don't like any of this. I just dropped her off last night. I get it, you got laid, but come on. Slow down!"

"I'm not doing it right now. I want to have it for the perfect moment."

His eyes narrow. "I'm only doing this because I'm worried you'll pick out something truly hideous on your own, like a pear-shaped, horrible quality diamond, in yellow gold. I'm not having that on my conscience. Fuck. You're going to propose today, aren't you? And they say *I'm* impulsive. This is a mistake." He opens the door. "After you."

We walk inside, and I spot my sister. I'm about to introduce them when Ethan chimes in, "Hi, yes, hello. *Wow*, I hope you don't mind my saying this, but you are positively enchanting." He shakes his head. "Anyway, we have quite the task today. This guy is looking to marry my best friend. I don't like it, but here we are. Can you help us find a ring that will impress her, but still be understated enough that she won't be embarrassed to wear it in public?"

Ethan pauses, waiting for a reaction. I can't help but let out a hearty laugh that he thinks she works here. Melanie is wearing a black business pantsuit and our mother's pearls. She dresses conservatively, which is typical for a corporate lawyer, but sometimes she overdoes it. I can see the confusion; she absolutely looks like she works here.

Enchanting? Is he hitting on her?

As entertaining as this is, I finally greet her. "Hi, Melanie,"

Ethan looks between us, and it isn't enough of a hint for him. He wouldn't be able to guess we are siblings—she looks like our mother, whereas I look like our father. "We have an appointment?" he asks. "Perfect. As I said before, this stale bagel needs a ring. What do you recommend?"

It normally takes a lot to make her crack but there's a small smirk tugging at her lips. "Dylan, who the hell is this?"

"This is Ethan, Emma's best friend, who I'm now regretting asking to come. Ethan, this is Melanie, my little sister."

"So... you *don't* work here? I should've guessed, but I see no resemblance between you two. You're absolutely stunning."

Yep, he is definitely hitting on my sister. Fuck my life.

"No, I don't work here. Dylan asked me to come." Her resting bitch face hasn't budged but she's... Shit, is she blushing? I absolutely regret inviting him now. There's some kind of stare down happening between them and it's incredibly uncomfortable. He better not get any ideas.

I clear my throat, hoping to interrupt their eye-fucking. "I asked you both to come to help me pick out a ring."

Ethan's gaze snaps to me. "I'm sorry, what?" He blinks twice. "I liked it better when she worked here. No matter how gorgeous she is, she is not qualified to pick out a ring for Emma. Are you sure you're related? She's..." Ethan gestures to Melanie. "And you're..." He looks me up and down like I'm bad sushi about to give him food poisoning. "But she has no idea what Emma likes. Why is she here?"

"Excuse me? I'm standing right here." At least the gross sexual tension between them is gone.

"She's here because I need a woman's opinion."

Now, Melanie's the offended one. "If you hadn't fucked things up the first time, you would already be married to her. You don't need a woman's opinion, you need to get your head out of your ass."

Shit, this was a bad idea.

"It appears we have more in common than I thought, princess." How is it Ethan and Melanie are both against me? Fantastic.

"Don't call me that," she spits. I never thought I would see the day someone got under her skin like this. I would pop some popcorn and enjoy the show if it was anyone but Ethan.

"Can we pick a ring? You two can fight about this another time." Luckily, they both listen and we go our separate ways to browse.

We wander further into the store to look at settings. These two find their way to each other and are bickering worse than my daughters—everything she likes, he hates, and vice versa.

I linger over one particular setting; it feels like Emma. They both come over to the case to see it, and thankfully both agree that it's perfect. It's the one. I pull out my credit card to buy it; the sooner we get out of here, the better. If they spend any more time together, they'll murder each other or hook up. I don't want to be here for either.

When I get home, I take the ring out of the box. It really *is* perfect and I know she'll love it. As soon as I talk to the girls about proposing, I'm going to ask Emma to spend the rest of her life with me.

27

EMMA
JANUARY

I've had more sex in the last few months than I have had in my entire life combined. Maybe that's an exaggeration, but it certainly feels that way. Dylan and I were together for almost a year when we were younger, but it was never like this.

Every weekend, we have a date night. Sometimes it's a movie, sometimes dinner or drinks, but when we get home, we're clawing at each other's clothes, unable to get naked fast enough. With our work schedules, and our kids... It doesn't leave me a lot of alone time with him. I can't help worrying this is going to be like it was with Jason.

Except this isn't Jason. While I'll always love him, I was never in love with him. My heart always belonged to Dylan. If we lived together, we wouldn't have this issue, but it's too soon to think about.

Since Dylan and I only have time to see each other on the weekends, we talk every single day. When the kids go to bed, he calls me, and we spend hours on the phone.

Surprisingly, we've never had phone sex, but I've definitely used my vibrator on more than one occasion after we hung up. Sometimes his sexy voice is too much for me to handle.

Jason has the kids for the weekend, so Dylan is taking me back to the mountains for an overnight birthday trip. We can only stay the night since he has to help Harriet prepare for her in-class debate next week. I love what a great father he is. He would never replace Jason as my own kids' dad, but I have from time to time wondered how Dylan would be as a bonus dad.

I pack my bag with a few of my sexiest outfits. Even though I'm sure he'll have me naked for the next twenty-four hours, it's good to be prepared. After hearing him come in my front door, I shout from the kitchen, "In here!"

My mouth waters as he enters the kitchen. He's wearing his glasses, perfect fitting jeans, and a henley tee that hugs his chest; he knows I find his glasses incredibly sexy, and wears them on purpose to get me all hot and bothered. Who knew glasses could double as foreplay?

There is so much intent in his gait. Once he reaches me, he cups my face and slides his fingers into my hair, resting his thumb on my cheek as his mouth crushes against mine. It's that hot hand thing you see guys do in movies and think *I wish my man did that!* Well, my man does. It's only been two days, but I melt into his touch as if it was so much longer.

Dylan lifts me onto the counter, and when I deepen the kiss, he lets out a satisfied moan into my mouth. With my legs on either side of him, I scoot closer until there's nothing between us. I bite his lip as I pull away, eliciting a rumble from his chest.

"Hey, handsome, I didn't even get a hello!"

"You wore those pants again, you knew the consequences."

"They're leggings, most women wear them. You wore your glasses, so I guess we're even."

He presses a chaste kiss to my lips. "I guess we are. You know I love you and as much as I want to have a quickie in your kitchen, we need to go, or we'll never leave your house." Part of me isn't opposed to the idea, but I've been looking forward to getting away.

I slide off the counter, and he grabs my bag before we make our way to the front door.

The drive is luckily uneventful. I was worried about weekend traffic, but we made it in record time. Dylan reserved a similar cabin to the one we had last time, and I can't wait to sit in the enclosed back porch that overlooks the lake, have a hot tea, and read a new book. It's my birthday weekend, and while my celebration may seem unconventional to most, any fellow introvert would agree that this is a significantly better way to spend their big day.

After telling him my plan on the way up, I'm not surprised as he jumps into action as soon as we get inside the cabin. With the last few months being so busy, I really need the day to do absolutely nothing. Within minutes, he's procured a couple blankets, two cups of tea, and our ereaders. I'm excited about the large porch swing; our cabin last trip didn't have one. We settle in, his arm around me on the back of the swing, and I curl up against his side.

Hours pass and we need to grab dinner. I didn't realize we spent the entire time out here until I check my phone. It's hard not to lose track of time when I'm reading but it's especially difficult not to when he draws lazy circles on my shoulder. It lulls me into a trance-like state. I love this man so much—he knows exactly what I need and is always taking care of me.

"I'm so cozy, but if I don't eat soon, I'm probably going to get hangry."

"Let's order something, so neither of us has to get up to cook," Dylan tells me as he kisses my temple and pulls out his phone. "What sounds good?"

"I honestly don't care. I'll pick something small wherever you order from."

"I'll order a pizza, so you can eat as much or as little as you want." He orders my favorite and goes back to reading his book.

It's getting chilly, even with the space heaters, so we wander back inside once dinner arrives. When we're done eating, still sitting at the table, he asks, "What would you like to do the rest of the night, birthday girl?"

I move from my seat and straddle his lap, combing my hands through his hair, messing it up a little. "I have a few ideas."

"Do those ideas include you getting naked?"

I nod enthusiastically, and his dimpled smile appears before I kiss it away. Dylan stands, taking me with him, and squeezes my ass, then playfully slaps it.

"Good. I'm going to spend the rest of the night buried inside you, baby."

"Best present ever. Happy Birthday to me!" I laugh when he smacks my ass again.

"You and that smart mouth of yours." His eyes narrow on me, shaking his head, before kissing me again and taking me to the bedroom.

"Oh, don't act like you don't like it. My mouth is quite talented," I tease between kisses.

"I like it a little too much." He sets me down on the bed. "I'll be right back."

Dylan loves to undress me, so I leave my clothes on. Less than a minute later, he comes in with a cup of ice. My brows pinch. "Ice? What do you intend to… *Oh no*. You're not going to freeze my nipples off!"

Taking off his shirt and tossing it on the floor, he commands, "Naked. Now."

Well, shit, if I knew he was going to go all alpha on me, I would have stripped down before he came in.

I slowly take off each article of clothing, giving him a little bit of a strip tease until I'm down to just my bra and panties I bought specifically for this weekend. They are lacy and completely impractical—perfect for driving him crazy.

"*Fuck,* Emma, when did you buy those?" Dylan doesn't let me answer, instead kissing my shoulder before pulling the strap down with his teeth. "You look so fucking hot in this, I almost don't want to take it off. But I have big plans tonight that require you to be *completely* naked for me." He unclasps my bra, taking it off and throwing it haphazardly to the side. Kissing down my chest until he reaches my peaked nipples, he takes one in his mouth, his thumb playing with the other. "Do you have any idea how irresistible you are? I'm fucking addicted to you." With his mouth on me, I can't get a coherent thought out. His lips travel down further until he reaches the apex of my thighs, kissing me though my underwear, and driving me crazy.

"Dylan, please."

My desperate plea feels unanswered as he slowly slides my underwear off and roughly pushes my thighs apart, making me gasp. "My greedy little minx." I love when he is on the verge of losing control. "So wet already. Is this all for me?" He takes a small ice cube, runs it up my pussy, circling twice around my clit, then takes it into his mouth. I quiver at the chilling sensation. "Fuck," he groans. "You're delicious, baby. I'll never get enough of you."

I can't help reaching down to touch myself. There's so much fire in his eyes as he grabs my wrist, stopping me. "No, you got to play with this pretty pussy all week, right now it's mine." Keeping the ice cube in his cheek, he lowers his mouth, slowly licks up my slit, then teases my clit with small circles. It's hot and cold at the same time. It's overwhelming.

My hands slide into his hair as I lift my hips up to increase the pressure and friction. "I need more."

"Then you better ride my face, baby." He says it so casually, but it isn't a suggestion, it's a demand. As he lays back on the bed, I straddle him without hesitating. "You don't stop until you come. I want you to make a fucking mess."

I used to be self-conscious about it, but he always insists that it's a huge turn on for him. I grind against his mouth as he sucks and licks my clit, hooking two fingers inside me where I need him. The pressure builds inside me, seeking release, but it's not enough.

Dylan murmurs against me, "Attagirl, just like that, baby. I know you're close. Let go for me."

The vibration from him talking sends me over the edge. One of his fingers presses into my ass and I come hard and fast, moaning his name. My vision blurs and I struggle to catch my breath.

"One more, baby, give me one more," he whispers, kissing the inside of my thigh.

That's new. Since when is he an ass man?

"No, I need you. Please." He takes off his pants, freeing his erection. I move down his body and I instinctively reach for his hard cock. "But first..." I look up at him through my lashes as lick from the base to the tip. He twitches in my hand as I swirl my tongue around the crown. I don't want to tease him, so I take all of him in my mouth until his thick cock reaches the back of my throat.

"Fuck, your mouth feels amazing." It's followed by at least ten more swears and praises. Then his hands are in my hair, but not to guide me, to pull me off of him. "Baby, you know the rules."

"Oh, come on. Please? It's my birthday!"

Dylan laughs and tosses me back on the bed, spreads my legs and massages my clit with the head of his cock. "No, your beautiful mouth isn't going anywhere near my cock again, until I've come inside you at least once tonight." The pressure is perfect, but I want him to lose himself in me. I grip the bedspread as he reaches to the bedside table to grab another ice cube, taking it in his mouth.

Dylan slides deep inside me with one, rough and claiming thrust. I'm so deliciously full. He sucks hard on my neck, and the cold from the ice cube causes my nipples to pebble and a shiver traveling down my spine to my limbs. I love when he marks me as his. Moving in and out of me, deeper each time, he places kisses all over my neck, shoulders, collarbone, and chest.

"Fuck Emma, your mouth is incredible but nothing beats having you wrapped around my cock like this."

He surprises me by pulling me on top of him. I try to push him back so I can ride him, but he's stronger and sits up, keeping his arms around me as I slowly sit onto his hard length. Once I'm seated all the way, he holds me in place.

"You're so beautiful when you give me all of you like this." He thrusts up deeper into me, and I surrender, letting him take control. As he rocks me back and forth on him, the grinding gives me the friction I've been craving.

I grip the back of his neck and pull his lips to mine. It's his deep, passionate kisses that I missed the last few days. It's slow and so full of the love he has for me. Every part of this feels so raw. I want to spend the rest of my life pleasing this man; loving him as much as he loves me.

"I'm close, please don't stop," I cry out and he keeps the same pace, thrusting a few more times until we come together.

"I'm giving you a minute to rest, baby. Then, we're going to have a little fun."

"What do you mean? Was that not fun?"

He chuckles darkly. "Of course, but there's something I've been wanting to do for a while. You trust me?"

"Of course," I reply as I feel him harden inside me.

That didn't take long.

"Your ass is mine tonight, Emma."

Wait, my literal ass? Oh… that explains some things.

He slowly pulls out of me and grabs a bottle of lube out of his bag, joining me again on the bed. "You're still so wet for me, but I want to be sure it's enough." In one swift motion, he flips me onto my stomach and tugs my hips up to meet him. A dollop of lube hits my crack as one of his fingers teases the entrance.

"Dylan, I've only ever done this with you. Please, be gentle. I know you can get carried away." I over my shoulder at him with a smirk.

His hand slides up and down my back as a growl erupts from his chest. "Really? You mean this ass has always been mine?"

"I've always been yours." He kisses my back and wraps his arm around my stomach, pulling me to him until my back meets his chest.

"But you were—"

"Married? Yeah, so were you. But you know damn well you ruined me for any other man."

He playfully bites my shoulder. "You ruined me for any other woman—no one could ever compare to you. No one ever will. I'm yours, Emma. Now, I want this beautiful ass, and I promise I'll be gentle." He gently moves me back onto my elbows, trailing kisses along my back. "I'm going to start slow, tell me if it's too much."

There's a familiar vibrating sound. "What is that?"

"I bought the same vibrator as the one you have at home."

Shit, that's not a bullet vibrator, it's a fucking rabbit!

He slowly presses it inside my pussy as he continues to play with my ass with one finger. "E, I want you to hold it in for me." I reach between my legs, and the sensation is incredible. "Attagirl, just like that. How are you feeling, beautiful?"

"It's… a lot."

"I'm just getting started, but I know you can take it. Just breathe for me. I'm going to put on a condom, because I want to finish in that irresistible pussy of yours." He pulls out his finger and rolls on a condom before he slips the tip of his cock in my ass. It's too slow, I'm being tortured.

"Dylan," I groan, "you need to move, I'm so close."

"Then come for me." He commands and pushes in another inch, then another, and another. I shatter, the cliché stars dancing behind my eyes. "You're a dream, Emma, taking me like this." I start to pull out the vibrator, but his voice gives me pause. "No, that stays in, baby. You can turn it down, but I'm not done with you. You're going to give me one more."

He pushes in all the way into my ass and I cry out in pleasure, "*Dylan!*"

"Fuck, I almost just came from hearing you scream my name." He slides out slowly then quickly pushes back in. "You were made for me, Emma." He thrusts deeper each time, and I fall apart, a wave of ecstasy washing over me, feeling drunk without a drop of alcohol.

Dylan slows his pace and I glance over my shoulder. Our eyes meet, neither one of us looking away. He pulls out, rips off the condom and tosses it off the bed, not caring where it lands, then reaches between my legs and takes out the vibrator, discarding it the same way. I already miss the fullness. His eyes are dark and full of desire. I break eye contact to adjust my arms but am flipped onto my back like I weigh nothing.

I wrap my legs around him, feeling empty and desperately needing him inside me. "I told you I wasn't done with you." I pull him to me and he slips in deep with zero resistance. "You're so fucking perfect." His rhythmic, controlled thrusts leave me breathless, moving in and out of me, deeper each time. I kiss him harder as he owns every part of me. "That's right, you're *mine*. Now, be my good girl and come with me." I was already close, but his words unravel me, both of us left panting as he empties himself inside me. Not pulling out, he gently kisses every inch of me within his reach. Between kisses, he murmurs, "I'm just going to live right here, forever. Is that okay with you?"

I chuckle softly. "I'm sure people would miss you."

"Not as much as I missed you all those years. I'm serious, it was always supposed to be you and me, beautiful. I want to spend the rest of my life with you… being buried inside you is just a bonus."

After what was easily the best sex of my life—or at least a close second—he remained inside me, his lips never leaving mine. Our kisses weren't rushed, but I couldn't get enough of him. I felt him harden inside me again, and after we shared one more earth-shattering orgasm, we took a long, hot shower, washing each other and stealing kisses. We spent the rest of the night in each other's arms, talking about the future and goals we have for work, our kids, and where we want to live. He's making plans, and every one of them includes me.

Waking up this morning, we're tangled up in each other, and I don't want to get up. "Dylan, what time is it?"

"It's… *Oh, shit!* E, we need to get up!" He scrambles out of bed.

I check my phone and groan. "It's only 7:30, I didn't think we needed to head out for another hour and a half. It's my birthday, can't I sleep in?"

"No, Ethan will be… he will be, um, waiting for us at home, and I, uh, told him we'd be early." Dylan is never flustered; he most definitely is right now. Something is up, so I sadly leave the cozy bed to appease him.

"It's fine, I'll text him right n—" He grabs my phone and I'm worried he is going to toss it in another body of water. "*No!* Please don't throw away another phone of mine."

Dylan holds it over my head, just out of reach; I swat and jump trying to grab it. "Just get dressed and meet me in the living room. You can text him later." Kissing my forehead, he walks out of the room, taking my phone with him. I can't work out why he's being so odd today.

I rummage through my bag and all I can find is a black shirt and my buffalo plaid pants. *Weird, I don't remember packing these. Where are all my sexy clothes?* I get changed, pack my bag and head into the living room, where I find Dylan in the kitchen making coffee, talking to himself... in matching pajama pants.

"Did you pack these?" I gesture between us.

He glances up with a smirk. Rounding the kitchen island, he pulls me into his embrace. "Happy Birthday, beautiful."

So, now he's calm? When minutes ago he was freaking out?

"Thank you." I lift up onto the balls of my feet to kiss him. "But what's with the pajama pants?"

Wrapping his arms tighter around me, he replies, glancing at his watch, "I have a surprise for you in... eight minutes."

"What did we talk about?" I hate surprises. I don't mind presents, but surprises are the worst.

"My fingers were crossed behind my back." I swat his arm and he laughs. "Okay, okay. I know, E. Have a seat on the couch, I'll bring a cup over for you."

This whole thing is so bizarre. I take a seat on the couch and he joins me with two cups of coffee. The moment he sits down, there's a knock at the door, and Dylan rushes to get up to answer it, muttering under his breath, "They're early."

As he opens the door, there are at least ten overly familiar voices shouting "Happy Birthday!"

I rush off the couch, knowing most of who might be here —Ethan, my boys, Charlotte, Riley, Lily and Andrew, their kids, Jason, Melanie, and Dylan's girls.

Wait, why is Jason here? In fact, why are any of them here?

"You guys! What is this?" I head over to greet all of them as they file inside.

Jason and Aiden hug me first. "Hey, Em. Dylan told me about a surprise he had for you. We wanted to be sure the boys were here for it. I know this is your first birthday since the divorce, but I hope you don't mind me being here with them to celebrate with you."

"Of course not! Thank you." I squeeze him tighter, before letting go. "I don't know what's going on, but I'm glad you're here." I am genuinely happy he's here with our boys. It may not be conventional to be good friends with your ex, but when have I ever been conventional? I'm dating my ex from almost two decades ago… Conventional and I don't mix.

Aiden is still clinging to my side. "Mommy, these pants are itchy." I glance down, then around to everyone. All of my friends and family—even Jason—have matching white and black buffalo plaid pants.

Dylan sidles up to my other side. He kisses my cheek and wraps his arm around my shoulder, then addresses my son, "You don't have to wear them, buddy. Your dad told me he packed you another pair of pants. Thanks for being a trooper, little man." He hugs Dylan and nods, my heart swelling at their small interaction. Jason pats Dylan on the shoulder with a soft smile, and takes Aiden into the bedroom to change. I am so thankful Jason encourages Dylan to be in our kids' lives, especially since my boys love him and his girls.

"This is so sweet. Thank you." I wrap my arms around Dylan's middle.

Ethan comes up from behind, sandwiching me between him and Dylan. "Is the threesome still on the table?" I look behind me at him and he wiggles his eyebrows at Dylan. There's some joke I missed, based on how they are both laughing.

"I fucking hate you. Come here." Dylan grabs Ethan into the hug, with me still stuck between them, and it's now a bit claustrophobic.

"All right guys, it's a little tight in here. You both are solid muscle and I'm a little squished." Dylan chuckles, kisses my forehead and releases us both.

"Thanks for coming, Ethan. Just try to be nice to my sister," Dylan tells him, eyeing him with suspicion.

How does Ethan know Melanie?

"Tell her to be nice to *me*. I'm perfectly charming, and a fucking delight." After wishing me a happy birthday, Ethan kisses me on the cheek and makes his way over to my twins.

"Okay, everyone! Mimosas are ready!" Riley calls out from the kitchen. The grown-ups head to the kitchen for drinks, while the kids are in the living room playing, reading, and laughing.

Charlotte flew all the way from New York, so I'm especially surprised she's here. "Char!" I wrap her in a hug, but am careful in case she's stressed from travel. "I don't know what this is all about, but thank you for coming."

"I'm actually moving back! I just need to find a place. Tyler said I could stay with him for a few days until I figure out something permanent. I wanted to surprise you for your birthday." I love her so much; it's the best birthday present that she's moving back here. We didn't grow up together, her mom married my dad ten or so years ago, but she's my sister all the same.

"You're moving back? Are you serious?" I squeeze her tighter. "You know, Jason mentioned his noisy neighbor was moving, maybe it's vacant?"

"Oh my gosh, that would be amazing!" she beams as she pulls back. "Finding an apartment has been brutal. I'll have to chat with him while I'm here."

"Thanks for coming. We'll have to get drinks after all of whatever Dylan has planned is over."

I wrap her in another big hug that's interrupted by Aiden bringing over a small present. "Mommy, this one says it's for 'my love'—*ew, bleh*—from Dylan, can I open it?"

Aiden and I take a seat and I look over at Dylan, who doesn't take it from him. Instead, he sits on the other side of me and tells Aiden, "If your mom is okay with it, you can unwrap it, but I need her to open it. It's her birthday gift."

Aiden nods and begins ripping it apart before handing me a small velvet box that screams jewelry. It's eerily quiet, and when I scan the room, I find all eyes on me. As I turn back to Dylan, he's no longer sitting next to me, but in front of me on one…

Oh, God. Is this happening?

"E, before you open it, I want you to know that we can take as long as you need for us to figure it out. There's one thing that I have no doubt about, though—I want to spend every day of the rest of my life with you." Tears sting behind my eyes as he continues, "Nearly seventeen years ago, you were my first love, but you're also my last. I've always been yours, beautiful. I can't go another day without asking: Will you spend the rest of your life as mine? Make me the luckiest man in the world and marry me?"

I cup his cheek and I whisper without an ounce of hesitation, "Yes."

As I lean in to kiss him, there's cheers and clapping all around us, with a, "*Gross, Mom,*" from Aiden.

Ethan calls out from across the room. "Open it! I picked it out."

Melanie smacks him in the arm. "You did not!" The way Ethan is looking at her right now reminds me of the way Dylan looks at me. If she's not careful, he's going to hoist her over his shoulder and carry her off into the woods to do all sorts of dirty things to her. There's something going on between those two, but I'll have to ask him about it later.

I open the box and it is absolutely perfect—if I could pick any ring in the world, this would be it. Dylan takes it out for me, slipping the beautiful ring on my finger. "The perfect ring for the perfect woman." I kiss him again but we're interrupted by my friends who want to see the new rock on my hand.

Noah and Charlie give me a hug at the same time and Noah asks, "Can we move in with Dylan now?"

"Um, we'll talk about logistics when we get home, but for now, let's just enjoy the rest of the day."

The answer satisfies them and they dash over to play with the other kids. Harriet and Lizzy give us both hugs and I'm thankful they are okay with all of this after what happened with their mom. Harriet assures us that she'll be prepared for her debate at school, enlisting help from Melanie and Charlotte to prepare for it.

After we enjoy the largest buffalo plaid pajama party to date, we begin cleaning up the living room, and help everyone get checked into their own cabins. Ethan is headed out somewhere, but before he does, he wraps me in his arms. "My darling, wonderful Emma. Since you're now going to marry a well gin and tonic—*when you're obviously top shelf, with extra lime*—I insist that you let me plan your wedding so it isn't a disaster. Can you imagine if he was in charge? No, you can't, because it isn't going to happen." Ethan is an incredible event planner, so he would be the obvious choice.

"How can you plan it when you're in it?" I cock an eyebrow at him.

He kisses my cheek. "Oh, my love, don't worry. I can do both."

I lower my voice and ask, "What's going on with you and Melanie?"

"Don't worry yourself with that. She may be the most beautiful woman I've ever met—other than you, of course —but she's off the table. I wouldn't want to upset *Mallrats* over there. Happy Birthday, Em." He winks, and I have to admit, Dylan does sort of look like a younger, hotter Ben Affleck. It beats Mayo as a nickname, that's for sure.

I step out of his embrace, and he holds my hand, squeezing once before letting go. Ethan leaves for the evening, most likely about to find a hot tourist while he's here. It's probably for the best, Dylan would probably kill Ethan if he tried to hook up with his sister; even if Ethan is one of the most amazing people I've ever known.

Once everyone is gone, the cabin is quiet, and we take a few minutes to finish cleaning up. As I am tying up the last trash bag, Dylan's arms wrap around me from behind and I melt into him.

"Thank you for today, it was the best birthday." I turn to face him, my palms on his chest. He rests his forehead on mine for a moment before picking me up until my legs wrap around him.

Looking at me with so much love in his eyes, he sighs, "Thank you for saying yes."

I kiss him softly, and as I pull back, I admire the new addition on my left hand. "I mean, how could I say no? It's so pretty!"

Dylan chuckles and pulls my legs tighter around him. "Need I remind you that you said yes *before* you saw it?"

"I know, but you know you could have proposed with no ring, and I would've said yes." He begins walking us to the bedroom. "Hey, we still need to clean up!"

"Not before I make love to my fiancée until she can't walk for a week." With a knowing look, he tells me the only thing I want to hear, "You're mine, Emma."

EPILOGUE — DYLAN
ONE YEAR LATER

"E, we need to go!"

"I know, I know! You try getting five kids packed for a weekend."

I am going to kiss that sass right out of her the minute she gets downstairs.

A year ago, I asked her to marry me. On the car ride home, I asked her to move in. A little backwards, but we decided to buy a bigger house as soon as we found the perfect one. While I didn't want to spend another night without her, blending our families needed to be done the right way.

I love our kids, and the life we're building, so fucking much. Noah, Charlie, and Aiden are my boys now, too. Jason may be their actual father, but they also call me 'dad.' He was the one that encouraged it. I'll never forget when he told me, "There's no such thing as too much love." I get why Emma maintains a strong friendship with him after their marriage—he wants what's best for his kids and for her. He comes over every Tuesday for dinner, sometimes bringing Charlotte, since she lives next door to him now. It's what I envisioned when I imagined a life with Emma—a revolving door of friends and family in our home.

Once we were settled in our new house, I began working from home. When Emma was promoted to President, I knew her time would be limited, and I wanted to be sure our kids had the best possible home life with all of the big changes happening at once. I love that I can support her taking on the literary world, and when she comes home to me and the kids, I can spoil her the way she deserves.

As it turns out, Ethan is one hell of an event planner. I was in awe at how he took everything Emma and I wanted and created the perfect wedding last fall. It was small, less than a hundred people, at the lake that's been our special place since our first trip.

Thinking back to my conversation with him over burgers, he must be a psychic: he was Emma's Man of Honor, I did indeed thank him in my speech for helping me win Emma back, and he even left with someone after the wedding. Only, I don't think it was a bridesmaid, because it was Ethan, Lily, Riley, and Charlotte in Emma's bridal party. Of my groomsmen, Andrew is married, and I know Matt is interested in someone else. It's because of Ethan that I get to spend the rest of my life with my first and last love, and he reminds me of it every time I see him. I don't mind indulging him. If it wasn't for his little plan to help me win her back, we might not be where we are today.

I bought Emma a cabin for her birthday and it was the hardest present in the world to keep secret. I originally intended it to be a Christmas present, but it wasn't ready in time. To keep her off my scent, I booked a trip for all of our family to spend Christmas in London, so she could visit Jane Austen's home and the kids could see all of the landmarks there. Harriet fell in love with the city, so we're now looking at colleges for her abroad. Emma insists it would be the perfect place for an aspiring YA fantasy author, but I'm not entirely comfortable with the idea of her being so far from home.

With the cabin finally ready, we are headed up there today, just the two of us for her birthday. I convinced my parents to take all of the kids for the weekend, giving us a much needed solo trip.

As we approach the resort, I glance down at my gorgeous wife napping on my shoulder. I didn't think it was possible, but I've fallen more in love with her every single day. Kissing the top of her head, I wake her. "E, we're here."

She shifts back into her seat and yawns. "Sorry, I fell asleep."

"It's okay, baby. We had a long week, you needed to rest." I take her hand in mine and squeeze three times before releasing it. "Let's go in and get our keys."

We make our way to the reception area, where most of the staff know us by name with how often we've come up in the last year. Our favorite, Tamra, is at the front desk greeting us. "Welcome back! I'll grab your keys in a moment, I'll just need you to sign a few things... Ah, yes, here we are. Since your cabin is lake front, we ask that no pets are brought with you on your trips. If this becomes a permanent residence, you can, but you'll need to pay an additional resort fee. Please sign here, and here."

"Um, I'm sorry. We don't have any pets... and did you say resident?" Emma asks with a frown. "You must be mistaken, we're just here for the weekend."

Well, the jig is up.

I tilt her chin to look at me and press a chaste kiss to her lips. "Happy birthday, beautiful."

"*What?*" She turns back to the desk. "I'm sorry, do we own a cabin? Did I hear that right?" She then mutters to herself, "There better be only one bed." Tamra stifles a laugh; it's become a running joke between these two since our first trip. Emma finally let me in on it, a few months ago, so I let out a laugh, too.

"No, baby, there are multiple bedrooms, so we can come up as a family, or by ourselves."

Emma is still stunned and muttering to herself, so I quickly sign the paperwork and get the keys. Once we reach the cabin, I set down the bags before opening the door. After I unlock it, I lift her bridal-style, and cross the threshold.

"Dylan, put me down, you're being obnoxious!"

"What? I've always wanted to do that! We missed the opportunity on our wedding night because I couldn't keep my hands to myself. When we bought our house, we had to wrangle all the kids. Now, I can cross it off my bucket list."

"And what else is on this mysterious bucket list?"

As I set her legs down, I keep her body pressed against mine. "Well, my beautiful wife..." I kiss her neck and whisper, "Let me show you."

The cabin has four bedrooms, so I converted one into a library for Emma and the kids. Holding her hand, I stop in front of the room. "Okay, close your eyes." I guide her into the room, and over to the ladder. I set her hand on it. "Open them."

Emma's eyes are everywhere in disbelief. "It's... Dylan this is too much. A library?" Her fingers brush the book spines on one of the shelves before she turns to wrap her arms around me.

"Do you have déjà vu?" A blush creeps up her cheek. "Where I..." I back her against a shelf. "Wanted you so fucking badly." Propping myself against it with my other hand, I bring my lips beside her ear. "I would have buried myself deep inside you, taking what's mine, right there in that bookstore."

There is a hitch in her breath before she replies softly, "I remember." She bites her bottom lip in anticipation.

I wrap my hand around the front of her beautiful neck, and gently bring her lips to mine. She moans into my mouth, causing my cock to press uncomfortably against my jeans.

"Now, be my good little wife and hold onto the ladder. I'm about to cross one more thing off my list."

LOVED MINE WITH EXTRA LIME?

I hope you loved reading Emma and Dylan's story as much
as I loved writing it! Wherever you feel most comfortable,
please consider leaving a review on Goodreads, Amazon,
or social media! Your honest review means the world
to me.

To keep up with all of my upcoming releases, be sure to
follow me over on Amazon!

xoxo,
Irene

ACKNOWLEDGMENTS

There are probably a million people I need to thank! I'll probably need exit music played by the time I'm through.

First, thank you to men who ghost women! This book wouldn't be here without you.

To the queen, Taylor Swift — I listened to the Midnights album no less than 50 times while writing this book, couldn't very well not thank you.

To my amazing alpha reader Shanae — thank you for being on this journey with me and helping me mold and shape this book into what it is today.

My fantastic friend and fellow author Amanda Bentley — there are no words. You inspire me so much and I am so thankful for your help with my books. I couldn't have done it without your daily voice memos and encouragement. Oh my gosh, I can say it now, I published a book!!!

Huge thank you to Marianne A. Scott and Emily Rath. You both helped me so much with your feedback with this book, I am so grateful for your time, especially since you had your own books coming out at the same time as mine.

Pssst! For anyone who needs books to add to their TBR, these books are so good that I had to talk about them in Mine with Extra Lime:

- Emily Rath — Second Sons Duet (Why Choose regency era romance)
- Marianne A. Scott — Made From Magic series (Romantasy)
- Brittanée Nicole — Falling for Whiskey Duet (Contemporary Billionaire Romance)

To my other incredible beta readers — Rachid, Michelle, Mary and Cynthia. All of your encouragement and feedback was so incredibly helpful! I appreciate you all so much in helping me give Emma and Dylan their happily ever after.

To my ARC readers — thank you for taking a chance on me! This is my debut novel, so you had no idea what you were getting into. Thank you for your excitement and taking the time to read and review it.

To my incredible editor H.M. Darling — I would be lost without you! Thank you for all of your help with this book!

To my old friend and very talented graphic designer, Robert Boord — thank you for giving Emma a glow up!

To @your.rayofsunshine, who was taking honey shots on TikTok Live — I promised you I would include a shot of honey in this book and I'm a woman of my word.

To my bestie, Melody — you're my biggest cheerleader and I love you to pieces! Thank you for listening to all of my dating stories in our 20s.

Finally, to my family — thank you for allowing me to live out this crazy dream I had. I love you all so much!

ABOUT IRENE

Irene Bahrd is a feisty Capricorn and one of the most avid readers you will ever meet. Her favorite genres to read or write include romantic comedies, political romance, romantasy, and the occasional contemporary or dark romance.

She started her writing journey as a dare from a friend, after recounting dating stories from her early twenties. They inspired her to write spicy romantic comedies and parodies that feature a variety of book boyfriends—though most are cinnamon roll golden retrievers. Many of her stories contain LGBTQIA+, disabled, and neurodivergent characters.

Irene can be found on most social media platforms under @irenebahrdauthor

ALSO BY IRENE BAHRD

<u>Top Shelf Romances Series</u>

Mine with Extra Lime

Falling the Old Fashioned Way

Royally on the Rocks

Trouble with a Twist

<u>Top Shelf Novellas</u>

Wine About It

Rosé to the Occasion

Mule Tide Cheer

<u>Love at all Cost Series</u>

A Voice Without Reason

Not Her Villain

Maybe in Fifty *(Prequel Novella to Unexpectedly Ruined)*

Unexpectedly Ruined

Sip Happens *(Novella)*

<u>Sapphire Lake Series</u>

Never Yours

Always Heated

<u>Needing to Score Series</u>

Kick Out of It

There is No Try

One Goal in Mind

Ready to Snap

Love & Politics Series

Arranged Vacancy

Absolute Majority

Accepted Precedent

Stand Alone ErotiComs

Flexible Standards

Royally Cuffed

Hard to Swallow

Holiday ErotiCom Novella Series

Merry in Spite

ForNever Mine

Summer of the Switch

Haunted Happenstance

Save a Horse

Stand Alone ErotiComs

Flexible Standards

Royally Cuffed

Hard to Swallow

Stand Alone Parodies

Divorce of Convenience

Expect the Unexpected Parody Novella Duet

Undeclared Heir

Undecided Heiress

Pelligini Crime Daddies Parody Novella Duet

Running from the Garden with Eden

Not My Bodyguard's Keeper

Magical Mischief Parody Novella Series

Unshifted

Uncharmed

www.ingramcontent.com/pod-product-compliance
Lightning Source LLC
Chambersburg PA
CBHW060359260626
47160CB00006B/2373